Take My Hand for a While

by

Larry Farmer

Cover Art by *The Wild Rose Press, Inc.*

The Wild Rose Press, Inc.
PO Box 708
Adams Basin, NY 14410-0708
Visit us at www.thewildrosepress.com

Publishing History
First Edition, 2026
Trade Paperback Print ISBN 978-1-5092-6458-2
Digital ISBN 978-1-5092-6459-9

Published in the United States of America

Dedication

To my beloved Harlingen High School
Assistant Principal, J Glenn Cleckler,
a proud World War II Marine
who survived the horrendous fighting on Iwo Jima

Chapter One

It was time to settle down. This dreaded thought nagged at me as I lugged my Marine Corps backpack to a better spot along I-10 to continue hitchhiking. No one hitchhiked anymore. Especially if pushing thirty years old. But this was part of life after growing up a rural Texan from the poorest area in America. We felt no shame in such. Nor as part of social dues from life in the sixties.

Yet these allusions were getting old with me. Cheap excuses. I was a bum who now felt like one. It was time to go home and get a job. Trouble was, I still wasn't ready for any of that. Just the thought of sitting behind some desk *nerding* my life away made me sick to my stomach. All these years later, the fears were worse than ever.

I looked the part of a cowboy. Six foot three, two hundred muscled pounds, dishwater blond hair. Gritty. Patriotic. Arrogant. Skeptical. I even had a cowboy name. Kaleb. All these things helped me define myself and made me proud. I joined the Marines back in 1970 to go to Vietnam with one big *kiss my ass* toward my flag-burning generation while doing so. Now, two years of backpacking around the world had added to my illusory résumé. No hippie freak from my Age-of-Aquarius domain had done any of that. I beat them at their own game, it seemed to me. My Marine Corps backpack accompanied me, as well as my short hair, to prove to everyone I was more Mike Fink than Bob Dylan.

These concepts of myself were true and bought me all kinds of time to get from Los Angeles to Texas in 1979. Or so it seemed to me. Except now it was too obvious that I was a bum. A college degree in Agricultural Economics at Texas A&M had greased my self-image too, except that nothing worked anymore. It was time to settle down.

The question was, how the hell was I going to do that?

Hitchhiking to Texas from LA meant hundreds of miles through the desert. Adventure didn't include stupidity. Not willingly, anyway. My Marine cartridge belt with its two plastic canteens was attached to the rear of my backpack. Emergency precautions were in order. Even that left me vulnerable to heat stroke, and some of the water might be needed to cool my head if exposed to much sun.

It is illegal to hitchhike on an interstate highway. Frontage roads that merged onto them could be used for it, though. Still, it dawned on me quickly how I hated hitchhiking. Must have slipped my mind. The adventures, the journeys, the places, the people—that part was great and greased my memories and gratifications. But to be stranded and alone out in the middle of nowhere? That sucked. Period. Perfect word. And some of the characters that picked up hitchhikers weren't always relishable either. It kept me nimble emotionally, however, to be prepared for anything. So these visions of being a knight of the road were gratifying.

Luckily, the rides were good from LA onward. Perhaps because of compassion for my plight, stuck out in the desert, the drivers were courteous and even sympathetic. I made it to the Arizona border by early afternoon. Phoenix wasn't that far away. Trouble was, unless a truck picked me up, a driver was liable to be going only as far as Phoenix, which would leave me stranded in a big city. All the more reason to stay glued to the freeway.

"How far you going, pardner?" a truck driver asked me later on at a truck stop as I refreshed myself. My backpack was good for displaying my hitchhiking agenda.

"Texas," I answered him.

This driver was muscular and without a potbelly. Rather young also. His overall appearance made me think he hadn't been driving a semi very long. He stared at me, in thought for a moment.

"I've got a delivery to a store in Phoenix. Then on to Tucson. Help me unload some crates when we get there and we can be on the road again half an hour after we arrive."

This might have been the reason he picked me up, but I didn't feel exploited. Earning my ride seemed appropriate.

"Sure," I replied. "Been a truck driver before. Not a semi or anything. And I grew up on a farm in Texas. I'm used to manual labor."

"We'll get to Tucson by late afternoon. You're welcome to stay at my house if you like. Just let me warn my wife that we'll have a guest."

"I'll be fine," I answered. "It's a long way to go still, to get to Texas, and a few more hours on the highway

3

would be nice if you could put me off in a good spot."

"Tell you what," he said. "I'll take you to a place on the eastern edge of Tucson. There's a restaurant where a lot of truckers stop to refresh. Some might be taking a break there before going on. That's not far out of my way."

"Thanks," I said gleefully.

A surge of energy rushed through me, giving me confidence at the thought of being around the so-called working class. Most of my rural background felt at ease with this. My parents survived the worst of the Depression and then the World War II years. Guys like the truck driver reminded me of my upbringing. They were the backbone of America to me. Doers. Workers. Survivors.

After we arrived in Tucson and did the unloading, he drove me to the restaurant he'd recommended. "Here, son," he followed up as I climbed down from the truck cab. He reached into his back pocket to fetch his billfold. "Here's a few bucks so you can get yourself a good meal. This restaurant serves good chicken fried steaks. You have a long haul ahead of you."

"No, sir," I chirped in reply. "I'm on my last segment of the trip. Been around the whole globe. I'll be fine the rest of the way."

He studied me and seemed to determine I needed the independence.

"Suit yourself," he said with a grin. "Good luck. Be sure to fill those canteens of yours. Prepare for the worst."

"Will do," I answered, giving a small wave of appreciation. "Thanks."

Chapter Two

"Hank's Cowboy Grill" was the sign at the entrance. A Johnny Cash song blared from the jukebox as I entered. This was my kind of place.

It was midafternoon and the restaurant was half empty. There were tables and chairs throughout, with booths at the walls and a long counter toward the front. There were many empty seats at the counter, since hardly anyone was using it, so that appealed. The young waitress handed me a menu, cast me a slight smile, then returned to placing dishes in the cupboards on the back wall.

The menu had good selections, but my mind was set on tacos. Surely Arizona would come closer to what I was raised on back home than those tacos I'd had in Bangkok.

"Are you ready to order now?" the waitress asked with a smile.

She seemed very businesslike despite the warmth that exuded from her. And now, looking at her, I was taken by her looks. Perfect height for a girl, perhaps five feet five. Probably a little over a hundred pounds. She had straight black hair that touched the upper portion of her neck.

"An order of tacos," I said, trying not to stare.

She seemed so "country" to me, in both mannerisms and demeanor. I missed home more now, just from being in her presence. She scribbled down my order on her pad, then turned to leave.

"Been overseas," I volunteered to her. "Wasn't sure how much things cost now. I've been gone a couple of years. Hitching home to Texas. Long journey ahead."

She nodded, then walked toward the kitchen to place my order. A jukebox in the corner aroused my attention while she was out of sight. It brought out even more homesickness in me, in fact. I wondered how many songs I might recognize. Surely, they had oldies on it.

"Wow!" I was reading the selections. "Buffy Sainte-Marie? She's wonderful! Oh, yeah! 'Take My Hand for a While.' Oh, man, it hurts so good!"

A broad smile creased my face as I stared at the jukebox in homage and soon began humming to the melody while listening to the words.

My waitress was setting a glass of water and some silverware onto the counter for me upon my return. She looked at me.

"I forgot we had that on the jukebox," she said warmly while placing a napkin next to my glass of water. "The owner here was going to take it off, a few months ago. He thought it too gloomy. I had to talk him out of it. My mom had it on an album, but a Glen Campbell album, not the original Buffy Sainte-Marie version. Mother played it all the time. I begged my boss to leave it on. Maybe by now he's forgotten it's there."

"Any tip you might have gotten from me went in the jukebox for that song," I joked.

"A tip well spent," she said with a smile and a touch on my arm.

I melted right there in front of her as I picked up my glass of water to sip, in the hope of distracting any emotions forming.

"I'm only going a few miles outside of town," the man at the counter three chairs from me said. "You told Mary Lou you're headed to Texas. That's two days away even if you get good rides. Three days if you're going much into it."

"Who's Mary Lou?" I asked him.

"That woman there, our waitress," he replied. "When she served me, she said you needed a ride out of town to a good hitching spot. It's midafternoon now. You don't want to get stranded in the desert, and that might happen to you if I take you with me and dump you where I'm going, just a few miles out of Tucson and all. There's a roadside park near there, though, and that's probably your best bet for getting a ride going anywhere."

"Getting out of Tucson would be wonderful," I told him. "Don't want to be stuck here. No money for a motel. Even a few miles out would let me camp out on the side of the road."

The man studied me for a moment.

"You're big enough," he commented, "but you may not be up to all the bad characters that pass through here. They'd take you for everything you're worth, even if you ain't got anything. If you survived them, there's still a couple or more deserts that would make you sorry you're alive."

"I just backpacked around the world," I replied defiantly. "Hardships come and go. I'm anxious to get home. I'll take my chances."

"It's your business," the man said sternly. "But it sounds to me like you've used up your quota of survival. But I'll give you a ride. That roadside park isn't far out of town. Only a bit farther than where I was going. There'll be some shade for you if you camp out. And some water in the bathroom they got there. I'll do that much for you, if you're so set on doing this."

"Appreciate it," I answered him. "Midafternoon is too early to quit travelling. I've got too far to go for such as that. So, yeah, get me out of town."

The man studied me again.

"Suit yourself," he said. "I'll wait for you to eat your meal and then we'll head on out."

I gave a nod with a grateful smile. Soon Mary Lou brought me my tacos. I took my time to eat them even though the man offering a ride was waiting.

"I'll take your hitchhiker you found, Mary Lou," the man said loudly as if for me to hear while she walked by us again heading for the kitchen. "There's a roadside park for him there. What d'ya think?"

She smiled approvingly at him, then glanced at me as if to see my mood.

After eating I followed my host to a rusting old panel truck in front of the restaurant. I put my backpack between us in the seat up front. He barely said a word along the way. Perhaps he was disgusted with my stubbornness or afraid to get to know me, since he feared the worst for me and my foolish mission.

The restaurant we'd just left was but a mile inside the eastern edge of the city. He drove nearly half an hour before we came to the roadside park he had mentioned earlier, well on the way farther east.

"Do you have enough money, son?" he asked paternalistically as I departed his panel truck. "It's not good leaving you here like this, but there is a bit of daylight left and maybe you can get a ride or two before

8

you have to bunk down. I'll leave you to yourself since you're so set on this."

"I'm okay," I said. "Thanks for your help. And if something bad does happen to me, I wouldn't want you to lose money because you gave it to me for a lost cause and all. I'm okay with cheap meals at cheap restaurants along the way. Greasy spoons. You know."

"Well, best of luck to you, then," he said good-naturedly while sticking out his hand to shake mine for supportiveness.

"My friends back home will be charmed by you when I tell them. Just your concern alone helps keep me company."

He nodded favorably at me again, then drove away. My surroundings looked promising and there was some daylight left. Nothing but arid bleakness all around, with a place to camp out that was off to the side of the road.

I didn't know what was worse, the scarcity of cars headed east, or that none of those that did pass by bothered to stop for me. I'd had worse luck hitchhiking before, but couldn't really remember when.

It concerned me to see the sun go down after a couple of hours while I was still standing there, cursing the cruel indifference of people to my plight. If there were no rides for me in the daytime, who the hell was going to pick me up now that it was getting dark?

A police car drove by. It slowed down a bit while doing so. The cop inside seemed to be scoping me out. A few minutes later he drove by again at an even slower speed. I wasn't on the interstate, nor its shoulder, but just inside the edge of the entrance to the roadside park. It was legal to hitchhike there. So why was this policeman so concerned with me?

9

Soon it was pitch dark. No one—but no one—was going to pick me up now. If they didn't pity a poor vagabond in desert heat, they would have no sympathy for someone on the side of the road, someone looking more shadow than real. I walked into the roadside park. Where would be the best place to unroll my Marine Corps sleeping bag? In such environments, I usually slept under a picnic table. Yet the night was comfortable, even warm and dry. No need for any roof, nor was there a desire to be too obvious, just in case a traveler pulled over for a breather. Better to sleep behind the table area.

Two pairs of headlights approached me from the highway, going very slowly. Both of them were police cars. I recognized one of them. The driver inside was the same one that drove by a couple of times, earlier. The cars pulled over in front of me. Three policemen got out of these two vehicles and walked menacingly in my direction.

"How long have you been here?" one of them asked me.

"Seems like forever," I answered while shrugging my shoulders. "At least two, probably three hours. I'm headed for Texas. That's where I'm from."

The three cops stared directly at me. They were wearing firearms.

"You have the right to remain silent," the one closest to me began. I stared at him, confused and dumbfounded, as he quoted the remainder of my Miranda rights.

They were arresting me.

"Empty your gear onto the ground," one of the cops said to me. "My colleague will inspect it while we frisk you. We're taking you to our precinct in Tucson for further questioning there. You'll be placed in a squad car, so we will need to bring your belongings."

After being frisked, I repacked my gear and then followed them, still rather confused about why they were apparently arresting me and taking me to their precinct. How was it better to spend the night in jail than to sleep inside a roadside park in an Arizona desert? But that was where we were headed.

"Put your things in the back seat," another policeman instructed. "Then get in beside them. We'll avoid handcuffing you if you cooperate. Is there anything you need out of your gear? Get it now, as we won't allow you to open it along the way."

I was placed in the car that had the two policemen in it. The other policeman waited on our car from behind us to begin the trek back to Tucson, then followed us once we were on the highway.

"What's this all about?" I finally asked once we were established on the interstate.

The policeman sitting in the passenger seat looked back at me. He seemed human and almost sympathetic as he gave me the details.

"There was a hitchhiker not far from here that got a ride with a truck driver," the cop explained straightforwardly. "The man slit the truck driver's throat and took his wallet with all his money. There were no witnesses, but there were those that saw this hitchhiker with the truck driver at a truck stop just before the murder. He fits your description and said he was headed this way. Same locale as you, same description as you. That's why we're here on our way to the precinct. I assume you don't have a lawyer."

"No, sir," I answered.

This was serious and made me nervous. But after all

my backpacking around the world, it seemed like just another adventure.

"We'll be at the precinct in a few minutes," the driver of the police car informed me as he glanced into the rearview mirror to look at me. "We'll take your fingerprints and look into getting you a lawyer. You said you were from Texas. Do you happen to have a lawyer there you could access? If not, we'll find you one here." He looked at me again in the mirror. "You say you were passing through. That you were at the roadside park where we found you for at least two hours. Where were you before that?"

"At a restaurant on the edge of Tucson," I replied. "About a half hour from here."

"So that would put you in that restaurant right at the time of the murder a few miles outside Tucson. Would anyone be able to verify you were there at that time? That would give you an alibi. We could check out your alibi before we book you. That's if there's anyone who could verify you were at that restaurant then for any length of time."

"There was a waitress," I answered. "She would remember me. We talked about a song on the jukebox."

The policemen looked at each other and seemed to approve.

"What is the name of the restaurant?" the driver asked. "We can get logistics to find it and we'll drive there. Do you happen to remember the name? It would help your cause."

"Hank's Cowboy Grill," I responded. "I can find it."

"That's not necessary," the other policeman replied. "Someone at headquarters will give us directions."

The driver talked on their radio to relate the details.

Soon an address was forwarded to them. They seemed pleased.

"Do you suppose she would still be there?" the cop in the passenger seat asked.

"I'm not sure," I answered. "But you'd think somebody would know."

"We'll find her," the driver assured.

Not much was said the rest of the way. The drive seemed to take forever. But then there it was, good ol' Hank's Cowboy Grill.

"Her name was Mary Lou," I told the policeman that had been driving us as he got out of the car to enter the restaurant. He turned to nod at me reassuringly. "She has black hair," I informed further.

The policeman was inside only a moment. The other police car was still with us and parked just behind us.

"You need to come inside," he said. "The waitress Mary Lou relates there was someone like you there before. She said she would know you by looking at you and asked if you could come inside. Bring your gear."

For me to bring my gear sounded like a vote of confidence.

"Yes, sir," Mary Lou said, looking at me with a warm smile. "That's him. He played a song on the jukebox that we both like, and that's what got us acquainted. He's a Marine. Not only that, but he left here with a guy that took him directly to that roadside park you found him at. That's where they were headed when they left here. No passing go, no collecting two hundred dollars." She snickered as she related the scene. "So he has two witnesses."

"You're free to go," the policeman told me. "You were not only cooperative, but you were surprised at our interest in you. That doesn't have to mean anything, but it did make you look innocent, how you really didn't know what our interest in you was about. You weren't acting. Most guilty people tend to overact. We'll leave you here. We're sorry we made you backtrack on your journey to Texas. It's dark now. You may be stuck here."

"I'll find my way," I replied. "I just came from backpacking around the world. I'm used to this. Well, not being charged with murder. But finding my way around somehow."

"It must be the Marine in you," the cop said proudly. "My son just joined the Marine Corps. I loved it when you explained how your backpack and combat boots were Marine while we were asking you questions on our journey."

"I understand," I said. "Y'all were very courteous and respectful. Doing your job."

"Good luck," the policeman said as he walked away with his cohort.

I glanced at Mary Lou, showing some embarrassment. "You saved my life," I said with a grateful half-smile.

"Just glad to help," she replied. "What's your name? We never introduced ourselves. Only talked about that song and whatever. And about how you've been going around the world."

"Kaleb," I replied. "And you're Mary Lou."

"How did you know that?"

"That guy that gave me the ride out of here told me."

"He saved your life just as much as me," she said. "I'm scared for you, just hearing all of this. It's so good we got to know each other. Well, not really know each other, but you know. Since it's nighttime now, Kaleb, the bustle is gone here and I'll be going to my apartment soon. Don't even think of hitchhiking anymore tonight. Especially with a murderer on the loose. I live in a very small studio apartment. No couch, just a lounge chair, so you'll have to sleep on my floor in your sleeping bag. But you'll be safe, and I want you safe. Be patient and have a coffee on me while you wait at one of these empty tables. Let me finish up, and I'll take off early. We'll walk to my apartment. It's not far. The streets are all lit up and it's safe or I wouldn't walk it every night."

"There's no way to express my gratitude," I answered back.

"Good," she said. "Don't thank me. It's special to have saved your life."

Our focus was directly on each other. Where it seemed to belong.

Chapter Three

I pulled a book out of my backpack and began to read while waiting for Mary Lou, sipping the coffee she bought me while doing so. After a couple of chapters, the intro to the song we liked so well played loudly on the jukebox. I looked up and walking my way was Mary Lou with a broad smile on her face.

"We can go now, Kaleb, but let the song finish first. Go ahead and put your book up, though. What are you reading?"

"A history of ancient Egypt," I replied.

She let out a chuckle. "This guy waltzes in here wearing a backpack and orders tacos. Then he reads books about ancient Egypt while he's here. What kind of world do you live in?"

"Don't ask," I replied.

"Grab your things. Let's go. Sounds like I won't be bored."

She led me out of the restaurant, through the small parking lot and on to the sidewalk in front, describing her small apartment as we walked, seemingly as much for something to do as to prepare me for my soon reality.

"This is it," she said as we arrived at her duplex apartment. Other such duplexes were lined up on either side of the one she rented. "It's small, like I said," she informed as if another warning.

It wasn't much bigger than a college dorm room. A

twin-sized bed was by one of the walls, while a small square dining table sat at the opposite wall with two chairs accompanying it. A scarred chest of drawers with a medium-sized television sitting on top of it stood against the far wall next to the bathroom.

"It's my castle," she said with a giggle. "You'll be okay for the night. There's a mattress standing in the closet for you. I don't have many clothes, so there's plenty of room for it and some other gadgets there. Some books, too, on the shelf."

She didn't seem embarrassed as she explained things. I wondered if she was so acclimated to her situation, or perhaps was from a family with some means so she felt this was only a temporary situation. She motioned for me to follow her toward the closet.

"There it is." She pointed at a mattress leaned up against the wall to our left. "It's a bit thin. That's so I can move it around. It should be thick enough for you, though, especially with your sleeping bag on top of it. You'll think it's a step up from what you've been used to."

"So, Waldorf arrangements for me, you say."

I slid the mattress out of the closet and into the middle of the room, then waited for her instructions for where to place it. She looked around the room as if to decide.

"Put it next to my bed," she instructed. "That's the most out of the way place in my small abode. It's like we're sharing a bed, except you're almost on the floor."

"Cozy enough," I replied.

She returned to the closet to fetch a sheet, perhaps to protect her mattress from my dingy sleeping bag.

"And now a pillow, too," she said, handing that to

me also. "Unless you prefer your backpack for a pillow."

"I might really OD with all this luxury," I joked, "and maybe not recover from it."

After laying the bedding on top of my sleeping bag, I glanced at her for what was next.

"How were you going to sleep?" she asked me. "Do you have pajamas, by chance? Ha."

My blank stare answered that.

"Okay, listen, I'm going to slip into my nightgown. Sleeping in ditches fully clothed must be commonplace with you, but while you're Waldorfing it here, you might as well take it farther and sleep in your underwear. I'm good with that."

"I'm suddenly feeling shy, though," I replied.

"Good," she said. "Some guys are anything but shy. You're making me feel more comfortable."

"So. Just peel off my jeans and shirt, then?" I asked.

"Why don't you go to my bathroom and change there. But take a shower first. Throw your dirties on the floor just outside the bathroom door. If you aren't in any hurry tomorrow, this complex area has a washing room, and I'll wash everything for you in a machine while we eat breakfast in the morning."

"That would be wonderful. I've got other dirty clothes from the last few days, too, if we're going to do that."

"Pull them out of your backpack, then. We'll put them in a trash bag. A clean unused one. Go on and fetch them. I'll store them, and when you finish with your shower you can just come out in T-shirt and underwear."

"Sorry, no more clean clothes," I confessed. "Except for some clean socks and underwear. Enough for one more change of those, but no more rugged clothes, now.

While I'm showering, let me hand wash the shirt and jeans I'm wearing now. They ought to be dry by morning."

"Okay," she replied. "It sounds like you've been living this way for a while. Hand wash it is, for the dirties you're wearing. Just come to grips with spending the entire morning here to do the rest of your clothes. My work begins at lunch. We'll get you fixed up by then."

She looked at me and smirked. Her attention my way felt domesticating. My few showers lately had been using the cold open beach showers on the shores of Hawaii. So my first warm shower in a week helped make me feel at home even more.

A nightlight plugged into the wall socket was left for me near the bathroom. I could detect her form lying in bed thanks to the dim light, while stepping over to my mattress next to her bed. She used an extra pillow so that, when she turned her head my direction, she could see me more easily. A quick glance her way showed parts of her figure in her green nightgown, which melted me. She patted the mattress on the floor for me to lie down.

"So why are you twenty-three and still going to a junior college?" I asked her, wanting to continue the talk we'd begun on the street getting to her apartment.

"To work my way through college," she replied. "To support myself, you understand. My father was killed in a car accident when I was eight. My mother is a waitress raising my younger sister and me. She can't afford to give me anything. I go to school part time on Tuesdays and Thursdays at the local junior college while working thirty-hour weeks or so at the restaurant. Between that and studying, there's a need to relax a bit, too."

Stories like Mary Lou's moved me. Not her plight,

but her resolve. Her resilience.

"If you have a college degree in economics like you said earlier when we talked, and were a Marine too," she pondered openly, "why are you stranded in my part of Tucson and spending the night on my floor and handwashing your clothes?"

"Do I seem foolish to you? Or maybe like a spoiled brat?"

"Not judging you, Kaleb, at least not yet. It does seem like a luxury, or perhaps irresponsible, for you to be doing this, though."

"I got fed up with my life."

"And so you prefer sleeping on my floor?" she asked with a bite.

"My parents survived the great Depression and World War II," I replied. "When it came time for me to fight our generation's war, a lot of our generation lauded the communists abroad while living in communes in America. Much of our generation hero-worshipped dictators who put their populations into work gangs and government factories. That wasn't enough. So much of our generation was into burning our flag. I joined the Marines to get away from them, except for never feeling it was far enough away. So backpacking around the world appealed. Just looking for my head, as they say."

"Boy, you're the ultimate rebel," she commented.

"Yeah, I did a one-eighty on our generation of malcontents, except it's worse than that. I was a computer programmer in Houston for a couple of years, and it was the worst experience of my life. Good pay in a prosperous city, but I hated money as much as any hippie. They don't really hate money, though, and I never figured out how to live without it myself, but

20

couldn't just waste any more of my life living for it. So, on to New York, then a flight to Europe, and on around the world. Just me, my passport, and my backpack. Happiest days of my life, in fact."

She turned onto her side while propping her head on her fist to look directly at me.

"That was a great twenty-five words or less explanation of a looking for your head scenario, Kaleb. I'm afraid to delve into it, though. Gonna need some sleep pretty soon."

"No energy to tell you more anyway," I replied. "It made you curious. Broke the ice. Nice getting to know you. We can sleep now."

She laughed.

"You're fun, Kaleb. And carefree. Your travels put a spirit in you. Probably already had some of that, since you related earlier while we were walking here how you grew up on a cotton farm and all. Then the Marines. A real scenario about home being where you hang your hat. Nice having you here, ya know. Glad we talked some through the evening to get us some background."

"Your floor of a bed is the best I've had in a long time. Thank you back."

"Hey, listen. Feel at home. Not sure what I mean by that, but relax while you're here. It's nice having you. I'm glad I don't have classes tomorrow."

"When do you leave for work?" I asked.

"On my days with no classes I leave here around eleven. That gets me to Hank's before eleven-thirty. That's when the crowds start picking up. Days with classes I try to get there before one."

"Well, listen, I need to be on the road by then. Don't want to get stranded."

She stared at me in silence for a moment.

"Kaleb," she said with a sigh. "Stay another day or so. Not just to wash your clothes. It feels good to have a man around here. It's been a while. And I'm not trying to sound like a come-on." She stared at me some more. "Or maybe I am. Wanting it to sound that way, you know."

This was sounding deep.

"Gotta get home, Mary Lou."

"No, you don't."

"Why are you so single, Mary Lou? You're obviously a bit lonely. Or game. And in spite of all the men you must encounter."

"My father didn't die," she said pointedly. "He left us. It's not that I hate men, but getting involved has no appeal to me. Being a waitress doesn't help either. A single waitress at a greasy spoon? There's some men think we're fair game. Or should be fair game, at least. I'm not being bitter, but that's why I'm in college. To get better than truck-stop predators. There's a lot of good working-class guys around, and a lot of disgusting white-collar saps, for sure. But at least the skilled and educated think they are supposed to answer to a higher calling sometimes. So, here's hoping education leads to a lesser of evils, you know. But hopefully to a lot more good."

"I'm a backpacker, Mary Lou. And a Marine and a hillbilly. I'm glad you let me into your apartment for the night, but why are you pushing it with me by doing so?"

"Because you're different," she said with a swoon. "You're so different. Good different. It's more than manners with you. It's like you really like people. And those you don't like, you can handle. Or so you seem to think. You have so much self-control and self-

22

confidence. And you're educated. There's a depth to you. Even when you're not talking, there's this vibration inside of you. The word 'depth' applies to you. So, build my self-confidence, Kaleb. Stay with me a while. Share your vibes with me."

She kept waiting for an answer, but I didn't know what to tell her.

"Sleep on it, Kaleb. I'm not putting the make on you. But I've got one night to get your attention. Just check me out for a couple of days."

I barely slept that night, though I needed sleep desperately. And finally had access to a mattress, thin as it was. But I pictured staying. She was attractive, with a good personality. She seemed intent on improving her circumstances. That impressed me. But suddenly she wanted me to stay, and that felt like she was intruding on me, on my life. I had a life. My own aspirations, whatever those were. Maybe I'd sort through all this after a good night's sleep.

What seemed like a few minutes later, there was a clashing sound that caused me to flinch with a sudden brightness inside the room attacking my eyes.

"Hey, Kaleb," a voice said from across the room. I cracked open my eyes. "It's rise and shine. You went into a coma. The sun's up now. You wanted to get on the road. I'll fix you some breakfast. Do you like scrambled eggs? Some bacon? With chopped onions and jalapenos in the scrambled eggs? Sound good to you?"

My eyes stared at her angelic figure. How was I going to leave an angel?

"Yeah, Mary Lou. Scrambled eggs sound good. Bacon sounds good. Thanks."

"Did you sleep well?" she asked.

"No, Mary Lou. No. Restless sleep, in fact. Until my coma anyway. You got me wanting to stay now." I twitched my mouth. "Sounds like I'm going to stay, then. We'll do my laundry, but then I'll stay longer anyway. Because of you, here in Tucson, Arizona."

Her smile broadened.

"Hey, don't get antsy, but I have a friend who owns a lumberyard nearby. Her father owns it, in fact. She and I went to the same elementary school, then on up through high school. Now she works for him in the office there on the grounds of the lumberyard. I called her a few minutes ago and she's going to find you a place there. Manual labor. You're big and strong and broke. Perfect. You're still a thousand miles from home. You're a survivor. Staying here is part of surviving too. Give it a shot. Am I being too bold? Are you going to survive me? It's my one shot, Kaleb. Hope you're game for a new adventure. I'm a good adventure."

A laugh came out of me that needed to be shared. It suddenly dawned on me I wouldn't miss this for the world.

Chapter Four

Mary Lou's telephone rang and she rushed to answer it.

"Yes, he's here," she said into the phone. "Do you want to talk with him?"

She listened to the other end intently. A broad smile came upon her face. She clenched her fist and pumped it into the air to celebrate, then looked at me with a wink.

"We'll be right there," she chirped. "I'll be with him to introduce everyone. Thank you so much. We're on our way."

Her joy showed and needed to be shared.

"Perhaps you can tell -- you got the job," she said with glee. "It's not too far. About a mile. I'll take you. There's a bus that goes there. You can take that in the future. Or walk."

I smiled at her and gave a quick nod of appreciation.

"Let's go now," she said, "to introduce you and situate you."

I concentrated on the streets and buildings along the way to get myself oriented so I could find the place without her help. It wasn't far, as was explained, but a bit of a walk, which is what I intended to do every day to get there. A mile up and a mile back, with eight hours of manual labor in between.

"Hello," Mary Lou said to a middle-aged man sitting behind the desk of an office inside the front building of the yard. "This is the Texan I told you about on the phone. As you can see, he's big and muscular. A farm boy while growing up in Texas. A Marine during the Vietnam War. He has an economics degree from Texas A&M and decided to see a bit of the world before settling down. We became friends and he decided to stay here a while with me before going back to Texas to look for more permanent work."

"So," the man said as he held out his hand for me to shake. "My name is Dale and I'll be your supervisor. Me and my dad own the lumberyard. My daughter works for me and is good friends with Mary Lou here, so that worked out for you. My dad's semi-retired now. We always need some help around here for the kind of work you'll be doing. I assume you've been told it will be mostly moving boards and blocks around. Loading and unloading trucks. We hire temps from a local agency at times when we need them, and I help out at times on the manual labor out back when the work piles up. You'll come in handy to fill in some of this for us. The pay is not much, for this kind of work. We have workers passing through here a lot because of it. How long do you think you'll be here?"

"A couple of months or so," I answered.

"As if it was a summer job, even though it's fall. Early fall. It'll be cooling off pretty soon. That will be good for you. We still have a bit of heat now."

"Yessir," I replied.

"So, you can start tomorrow?" Dale asked.

"Yessir. Mary Lou is helping me catch up on getting some personal things done. I'll be ready tomorrow morning."

"Okay. Be here by eight in the morning, then.

Looking forward to having you."

We turned to leave and remained silent until outside.

"It's barely above minimum wage," I said to her as we walked to her car with the full brunt of starting work sinking in. "Forty-hour weeks. Lifting heavy objects. It's like I'm back in Texas."

"You're big," she said encouragingly. "You have free rent with me. Let's go get our new mattress. I need you with me to make sure we get one long enough."

"Let me help pay for it," I offered.

"It'll be mine when you leave. I'll stick it under the mattress already on my bed whenever you go back to Texas. Good for guests and better than my floor for them. So."

"I'll at least help pay for the rent."

"We'll see," she replied. "When you get paid, we'll see where things stand."

Mary Lou placed her arm inside mine as we walked to her car.

"I have the business card for here," she told me as we walked. "Leave early tomorrow so you don't get lost. He'll probably be understanding if you get lost getting here on your first day, but still."

"I'll be by myself," I said as we entered her car. "While you're at work today, I'll walk here to make sure I know my way. It's far, but it's also direct from your apartment, plus I have the address on the card you just gave me."

"It's a bit of a walk," she said.

"I do more than that just hitchhiking sometimes."

"That's probably true," she said with a smile. "And you're a Marine."

She seemed pleased with that aspect of me.

"So, Kaleb," she said as she turned the key to her car. "Your clothes are surely dry by now. I hated leaving them in the washroom dryer, but I've got to go to work rather soon and we had to get your clothes done. To make you human again. We'll take them to my apartment when we get there. Then some lunch. Something for both of us to go on for the afternoon. Then I'm off to work."

"If I'm going to be here a couple of months, I should know where this Hank's Cowboy place is where you work. Where we met. Just to know. I haven't a clue how I got there before, really. I was dropped off there. Not that I want to disturb you at your workplace. It's just that I'm still not sure of my way around and don't remember how I got there before."

"We'll get to all that," she assured. "Let's settle for learning how to get you to work and back to my place for now. Then we'll branch out to other things."

We arrived back at her apartment after grabbing a hotdog from a nearby stand. Together we fetched my clothes back to her apartment from the washroom, and then she left me to myself while she went to work at the restaurant.

"It will be eight tonight before I come home, you know," she said as she opened her door to leave. "You gonna be okay? You know how to turn on the TV. And you have your book on ancient Egypt. Don't get too bored. Things will get better once we catch our breath from all this new stuff in our lives. In the meantime, stick our new mattress on top of our bed. You'll sleep with me tonight. Forget the floor. How's that for new adventure?"

My serious expression showed.

"Thank you for everything, Mary Lou," I said softly, displaying my vulnerability. "You saved my life, put me

28

up, found me a job. Now we're sleeping together. I want to make you happy."

She looked me straight in the eye. "You already have, Kaleb."

Chapter Five

"How was your first day at work?" Mary Lou asked me as we lay on our new mattress together the next night.

"Dale's a rough character," I answered her in the darkness. "He's nice enough. And he really likes Marines. He told me that's why he hired me. Because I was a Marine. He needed someone, but not that badly. They were getting by, and the temp agency fills in okay for short-time help. But I'm big and muscular, a Marine, and working for a pittance, so he hired me. He asked a million questions about the Marines while we were working. One of the helpers out in the yard was showing me the ropes, but Dale came out to work with us just so he could talk to me about the Marines. That's my impression anyway. I'll take it. I took enough grief from our generation for being a Marine, so it was kind of nice to be around someone so in awe of us."

"That's good, Kaleb," she said as she stroked my cheek affectionately in celebration of my first day on the job. "You're comfortable here, it sounds like. But you know, you hardly have any clothing. Just how did you go around the world with nothing more than that to wear? It's like you had the clothes you were wearing and a spare or two extra, and that's it. You didn't have access to washing facilities every day while you were off backpacking, so I dread the thought of your situation as you wore the same clothes over and over while trudging through third world countries and sleeping on trains and in ditches."

"Farm work growing up was gritty, you know," I answered her. "We had washing machines available, so we washed every day, and there were plenty of work clothes, but the days were long and dirty. So it wasn't just all new to me to live the way I've been the last two years. And I wasn't traveling all the time anyway, during those two years of backpacking around the world. I lived some in England, Switzerland, Germany, Israel, India, Taiwan, Korea, and France. All places where I could take better care of myself. Even on the road I'd go to a hostel for a night sometimes and hand wash everything in the sink or in the shower."

"You got by, huh?"

"So to speak."

"So to speak indeed, Kaleb. But they are interesting stories. The stories you've told so far, anyway. And now you're stuck in Tucson while living in a shoebox with me."

"Our shoebox is cozy, so who cares?"

"You like me, don't you, Kaleb?"

"Is that a trick question?"

"You never tell me words of affection. We've got to where we hold hands now. We haven't made love yet. We kiss, though."

"I don't want to make love yet, Mary Lou. Guys are always pouncing on girls. You saved my life. Perhaps even literally. Let me make you happy, grateful that you did."

"Well, you know the answer to that. Because I keep telling you and showing you. We should trust what we've become. Not that we've become anything, but...

you know. We're openly affectionate around each other now. It's nice. I've had issues with eager boys before. You show me so much respect, and it melts me. Who is this guy? You're grateful to me for saving your life and putting you up, but it seems to be in your character to show respect to others. It seems natural for you, even if I'm special for some reason."

"I've had girlfriends before," I answered her deliberately. "Even in these places where I've traveled. Girls are endearing. I know we're geared to replenish the earth or whatever, but girls are so wonderful. Except for those that aren't."

"Except for those that aren't?" She snickered. "There's some stories there."

"Yeah, yeah. There are some stories there. But it's so easy to like girls. They are wonderful. Women are innocent until proven guilty. I've pestered some women, though, at times. There's so much biological pressure. These replenishing-the-earth hormones mean business, you know. They are ruthless at times. I've had to struggle with it too. To find ways to leave girls alone from it. It didn't come easy, holding back my urges."

"We'll get into all of that about those women that aren't so innocent and also about your biological urges," she said. "But it would shatter the mood. And for the last two days now we've been together. We're on a roll and I'm enjoying it. Maybe it's karma for me, being a damsel in shining armor. Who knows? But we've connected. And since I've got some stories about guys that aren't so great, I'm grateful to you too. Yes, Mother Nature geared people for whatever reason to find rapport and fall in love and replenish the earth, and now here we are, caught right in the middle of it."

"Not to get off the subject, Mary Lou, even though it's starting to get a little too deep. We've still only known each other for two days, so let's breathe and be human first. Mortal human, you know. Not shining-armor human. While you were gone to classes and then later when you were at work, I walked around the lumberyard area and all, just to get a feel of the place. Then after work today, just walking around, you know, there was this karaoke place or something near here. A little past the lumberyard. Right in that area. Just to acquaint myself with my environment, I was walking around, like I said. A little past the lumberyard there's this karaoke place. They not only have customers sing to karaoke and such, but they also have real singers performing on stage with a band or perhaps singing solo with a guitar. Some were pretty good. Some weren't. Especially bad were some of the karaoke singers. It's amazing how some people think they can sing. Anyway, they have prizes. I'm thinking of entering, but I need a guitar. So come payday I'll get myself a cheap guitar, used or something."

Her eyes lit up.

"There's a guitar here," she said. "In my closet. I'm surprised you didn't see it. It was behind the mattress you pulled out the night you got here. And also when you put the same mattress back in the closet after we bought the new one. Hmm. If you're going to enter that contest, that means you know how to play, then."

"You have a guitar?" I asked excitedly. "Seriously? Yeah, I know how to play! So many people back home are into songs and such, just to pass the time. My hero is Hank Williams. It's a rush, knowing we met at *Hank*'s Cowboy Grill. Fate, somehow."

"The place was named after Hank Williams," she replied. "Hank Williams is the Hank on the sign. There's a story about it. That place started off as a honkytonk years ago. Decades ago. They served snacks and beer and had local bands perform. Tucson and the times outgrew such hickness. If you ever go to the restaurant with me again, look it over. At the back wall there's about ten yards of an old stage. The owner uses it for storing extra tables now, or whatever. Bands back then used this old small stage. The owner used to have the customers pay their bills and stuff there too. But he prefers they do that at the entrance area, anymore. The stage is there still, even though it's not used anymore for anything but storage. The honkytonk used to be called Hank's back then, too, after Hank Williams. The new owner, my boss, kept the name, hoping to keep some of the old customers, even though now it's just a restaurant."

"A restaurant with a jukebox," I added.

"Exactly."

"But back to reality, Mary Lou. You said you have a guitar."

"Oh, right. We got off the subject." She got out of bed to fetch it. "It's just right here. So, wait for me." She looked back with a wicked grin. "You're going to sing to me. Maybe I'll fall in love with you after all."

Soon, she brought back a beat-up and scarred guitar. The strings were corroded.

"What am I supposed to do with that?" I groaned.

"Sing me a song, remember?"

"Yeah, right. Ha."

She handed the guitar to me to strum just to get an idea of what sound might come out of it. It wasn't just out of tune, the corroded strings made it seem *hopelessly* out of tune. They produced more of a thud than a chord. A few of the tuning posts used to tighten the strings were broken and some of the pegs, too, so tuning it would be a major challenge.

My dismay showed. I did not have much confidence for my debut, even with Mary Lou as a devoted audience.

"The neck's a bit curved. Warped. You left the strings too tight through the years. You're supposed to loosen the strings if you leave a guitar sitting around very much. Do you have a pair of pliers, Mary Lou? And some oil?"

"Yes," she answered. "And a crescent wrench too."

"Just the oil and pliers."

For several minutes I toiled with the strings and pegs, but couldn't get it fully in tune.

"Speaking of Hank," I said as my singing introduction to her, "this is one of my favorites. And it's a knights-of-the-road type of song, too."

Humming the melody to myself helped me find the chords to fit the song. Chords grossly out of tune. But Mary Lou remained starry-eyed.

"That was beautiful, Kaleb. God, that was so beautiful! That was a Hank Williams song? He wrote so many."

"It's called 'Rambling Man,'" I said.

"But 'Rambling Man' was an Allman Brothers song," she informed me. "Oh, but theirs was a different song, somehow."

"You can't copyright a title."

"That was hauntingly beautiful, Kaleb. Wow. I gave you benefit of the doubt that you were probably an okay singer, a country boy from Texas with other country boys that sang around campfires or whatever while growing up. But you were wonderful."

"Entering one of those contests at the karaoke place really appeals to me."

"Oh, yes, Kaleb! Oh, yes. Oh, yes. There will be other country-type singers that go and sing there. But yes, yes. You have to enter. We've got to get you a good guitar, though, so you can practice. Let's go to a couple of contests, too, to see what we're up against. Kaleb, I'm trying not to fall in love with you. Like you said, this is just our second day together. We can be affectionate. The affection we share is fulfilling. But no falling in love with anyone. Absolutely forbidden. A waitress and a part-time college student here. I've got to get my life in order first."

"Okay, okay, Mary Lou. Got it. Then we won't fall in love. But I'm not holding back, either. If that's where we're headed, let's go. Another adventure on the way."

"This one together," she swooned while kissing me passionately.

Chapter Six

"Where'd you get that guitar?" I asked Mary Lou as she drove me to a music store during my lunch break. "I mean, you live in this shoebox, with few possessions and no room for the few things you have. Yet there's this beat-up guitar shoved behind a spare mattress in your closet. What gives with that?"

"It was my father's," she answered. "That's all I've got left of him. The good him. He dreamed of going to Nashville. We even wondered if that's where he went after he left us. Chasing one of his dreams. One denied him by settling down and getting married to my mom. He used to sing to us. Mostly Carter Family or Roy Acuff, but Hank Williams too. Others. Some Gospel. He was religious. Except for deserting his family. Anyway, that old guitar helped fill in some gaps in my heart after he left us."

"It's almost sacred, then," I said in sympathy. "Yeah, my father sang, too. He was a cotton farmer from west Texas. Came home from the war after he was a bomber pilot—World War Two, not Korea. He married my mom, the homecoming queen where they grew up, not Lubbock, but Lubbock area. You've probably heard of Lubbock. So he came home and bought some land in south Texas. The exact opposite of west Texas, farm-wise, anyway. Land with rich black soil and plenty of water available. You can dig a well from attainable water levels under the ground for your crops or access abundant water from irrigation ditches attached remotely to the Rio Grande River nearby. He wanted to be a country singer when he was growing up. It was a ticket out of the Depression. But after the war and with a new bride, he bought a farm with the GI Bill instead and gave up all ideas about singing in Nashville, though he still sang in church. He had a good voice and used to get requests from the congregation. Solos, I mean. He loved to sing for the church with solos. I was proud of him."

"Was he as good as you?" she asked me.

"I don't know. I sound different than him. Not sure why. It's not like I took after my mother. She couldn't sing well. So much so she didn't even bother to sing in church. She didn't just not sing solos, she didn't even sing along with the gospel songs at the beginning of the services. We'd sing forever, those days in church. In the spirit. I love gospel music to this day because of the services and my father. He'd sing at home too. Came in from the fields and would sing instead of watch TV. I loved it."

"But you never had dreams of Nashville, it seems."

"No time. College, Vietnam, backpacking around the world, whatever. So much adventure in my blood to contend with and needing to get it done before settling down."

"But that doesn't make sense," she challenged. "You're thirty years old. It's one thing to get away for a while. To find your head, as you say. But you're ready to lock yourself out of everything, Kaleb. Out of a job and family."

"There's a world out there, Mary Lou. Don't know what else to tell you. I have a college degree. And I could have taken over my daddy's farm. But any thought of settling down got me antsy, feeling stuck, especially when I lived in Houston and was so miserable. There was some Davy Crockett fixation inside me, the allure of far off places. I thought about homesteading in Alaska after getting out of the Marines. Except by the time I applied, there were land disputes with the native Indians and Eskimos. I nearly emigrated to Australia, too. They were even giving farmland away to people like me, trying to lure us there. Adventure! Adventure called me. Plus all this disgust with my generation. I believed in the Vietnam War, but that wasn't it. There were reasons to fight or not to fight. We all had to make up our own minds about things. But our generation just seemed like spoiled brats. They seemed glad there were good reasons against the war. Anything to not serve their country or fight tyrants. It was the fad for a while to carry around Mao Tse-Tung's little red book. They made a hero out of Ho Chi Minh. I mean, he was a nationalist and all, so that part is understandable. Watergate was going on, so we had corruption on our end. There were causes to understand about my generation. Racism and Jim Crow laws were going on, too. America definitely had faults. But the hippie movement and the antiwar movement just seemed like cults to me, and spoiled brat ones, to boot. They didn't have any answers for me. And traditional America didn't have enough answers for me, so I wanted to fill in my own gaps. Traditional America was at least home to me. But I needed to look for my own answers. To go my own way."

"But you lived like the hippie crowd for a couple of years."

"Some things about them held appeal. But Davy

Crockett appealed to me more than drugs, sex, and rock 'n' roll. I didn't mind questioning things, but that included questioning things that disgusted me about my generation too. Hippies especially."

"Oh, Kaleb," she said with a giggle, "you're a character! But here's the music store now, so let's go inside. They've got guitars in this store. All kinds, though our choices are limited, since neither one of us has any money."

"Just something to learn songs I already know, Mary Lou. Get myself oiled again, so to speak, presentable. Then audition and hope for the best since I don't have a band. That's why that karaoke club appeals."

"Does anyone care anymore about a solo singer with a guitar?" she fretted.

"No idea," I answered as we walked into the store. "I was a hitchhiker, and then I met you. On a roll here. That's what I know."

She nodded with a jerk and seemed pleased she was part of any quest of mine.

There were no cheap guitars in the shop, not for our budget, at least. But some were cheap enough to purchase.

"There's still time before we go back to work," she said as we walked to her car with our new guitar. "Let's listen to a song from you in my apartment, and then I'll drive you to work before I go to my restaurant. Let's go back and let me hear you break this thing in before work starts."

Tuning it took more time than we had. We would both be late for work, but I had to get in one song on my new prize.

"Dream," she said with a swoon. "Everly Brothers.

Good enough to break in with. It's an oldie but simple."

We became glued to the song with my guitar accompaniment, easy as it was. I could do this.

"Come on," she prodded me. "We're only a little late for work. We'll use the usual excuses. I'll drop you off first. No one better play the jukebox today, so this song can stay inside my head for a while. I may dance while serving my customers."

She ran the stop sign at the corner since there was no traffic around. The lumberyard had no customers in the parking spaces in front of it. Hopefully, the owner wouldn't notice my tardiness as I jumped out of her car and ran to one of the sheds.

"You're ten minutes late, Kaleb," a voice behind me said. It was Dale. "This isn't the Marines, but punctuality is still a requirement."

"Yeah," I said remorsefully. "And I'm new here. Not good. It won't happen again."

"I'm sure not. We had a load of some cedar planks. They're piled up just in front of the pine logs. You'll see them. You can handle them yourself. I've got to see a man that wants some plywood. I'm taking Jose with me, so you'll be here alone. I expect the planks to be stacked on top of the others we have out there. By size, of course. We won't be long. You'll need to sweep out the small shed at the back when you finish stacking. That'll keep you busy."

It felt good to be alone. Nothing to disturb me while working. I could daydream in peace about my guitar and the karaoke that night.

Chapter Seven

The joint that held karaoke contests seemed more like a coffee house than a bar. In fact, there was almost as much coffee and soft drinks being served as beer. Sandwiches and dips were available as if accompanying any beverage.

Mary Lou and I took seats toward the back. The lighting was minimal, as if to draw attention to the stage.

"We haven't missed very much," Mary Lou noted.

"It doesn't matter. I just wanted you to get a feel for the place. Absorb it and acclimate so you know what you're getting yourself into."

There was no emcee. Just a man at the side of the stage where the contestants stood in a waiting area. When a singer finished, they simply walked off to the opposite side of the stage from where they'd entered it. The stage manager then waved on who was to be next.

Some of the contestants played only musical instruments. If it was a piano piece, they pushed out a small keyboard on rollers. One man did animal sounds, another yodeled. Everyone else sang. Occasionally, there was a duet singing, or a trio.

"You can match them, Kaleb. Some were pretty good, but not better than you."

"I'd feel like a clown out there, Mary Lou. They looked clumsy."

"That girl singer was pretty good," she countered.

"She had the sweetest voice, and her guitar arrangement backed up the song so well. Maybe she'll win."

"How do they decide who wins?"

"There was applause, as you noticed, immediately after each performance. But also they'll be reintroduced one at a time at the end of the night. Everyone's had time to evaluate performances by then, and so the audience votes with an enthusiastic applause or not when each performer is reintroduced one at a time. The owner decides from the applause who won. That gets a bit ridiculous sometimes when you can tell he's prejudiced for someone. So he limits any favoritism, to keep people happy. I've only been here a few times, and enjoyed it, but it gets old to me quickly, so I don't come here much."

"Aaahhh," I groaned. "I don't want to do this."

"Just give it a try, Kaleb. Suck up your pride for a night."

My squirming answered that suggestion.

"Just give it a try," she repeated.

"I'll think about it," I said.

"Good. Make me proud. It'll be a good memory someday. Even if it is so amateurish. It's fun for these people here in the audience. As if they run things too, not just the owner. It keeps them coming back, sometimes just to laugh."

We stood up to leave. This was why I didn't want to be a singer in the first place. I'd felt almost raptured from hearing a Hank Williams song at times, through the years, and would dream "what if..." But show biz sucked. Nights like tonight reminded me too vividly.

All the stupid things people did to get discovered. Some amateur with a dream. It didn't always work out. But Mary Lou inspired me. Just get the guitar and start singing, I told myself. No need to be a fool. Competitions were often fun. A learning experience.

If I was going to do this, it had to be my way. It wasn't worth chasing rainbows. Sink or swim was going to happen, so I needed to just be myself.

"You're singing," Mary Lou remarked as she came in from working her night shift later that week.

"I love this guitar," I answered. "It's tuned comfortably for my key. I've worked out songs I learned back home while growing up."

She stared at me for a moment.

"How do you enter this contest?" I finally asked her.

"We'll find out," she said. "You won't be embarrassed, Kaleb. It's good to worry about things like that. Any professional would. And should. But you won't be embarrassed. Some of the performers are good at these outings. Be like them or better. What are you going to sing?"

" 'Lovesick Blues,' " I answered. "It's a hard song to sing. It's got these little yodels in it. Not the complicated kind, but mostly a falsetto slur on some of the words. It's got a good beat and melody. Good imagery. It's innervating. If you do it well, it's captivating."

"Have you sung it to me before?"

"I don't always do it well and was embarrassed for you to hear."

"Why would you be embarrassed? That almost hurts my feelings."

"It's not fair for me to say that to you, for sure. But now you know. Be warned."

"Okay. I'm waiting for the day. But while you're going over old songs, be sure you prepare more than one song. You need options. Let me make some coffee, and I'll put something on the fire for us, too. We're finished for the night. Let's hear what you've come up with now that you have a guitar. Just for me. We're still getting to know each other, so we'll add some depth here and now, with this."

The problem with singing in front of her was that it let the genie out of the bottle. Once I was singing, it was like an eruption inside of me. I didn't know how to quit.

"Kaleb," she whined after more than an hour of hearing me sing my songs. "It's enough. I love it, but it's almost midnight. We have to get some sleep. We have to go to bed. My God, how have you survived all these years of not being a singer? You're a natural, including your obsession. But it's bedtime. We have to go to bed."

I laid the guitar against the lounge chair and got up. Indeed, how did all these years go by in my life with me not obsessing to be a singer? Two years backpacking explained some of it. Backpacking was at least something else to obsess about.

The snuggling we did that night was the best ever. We woke up in the same position as when we dozed off, hugging each other forehead to forehead.

This part of my life was the place to be. A different verse from what was going on during the last two years for me while making my way around the world backpacking. Mary Lou made it so, as did acclimating to life in the lumberyard. Though work was tedious and demanding, Dale was fun to work for, even as grouchy as he insisted on being. And I got to know my coworker in the yard better, too, as we bonded more every day.

"I grew up on the border," I related to my workmate Jose. "We hired a lot of illegals on our farm."

45

"So many come as farm laborers," he replied, "from Mexico. And laborers like me. I wanted better. That's why I'm here working for Dale. It's better to toss boards than chop cotton or pick it. The money is better, too. Except that I had to find a place to live while here. On a farm the *patrón* provides a shack."

"How do you speak such good English?" I asked him.

"It's called survival, *hombre*. Work on a farm doesn't need English, but for the better jobs I better speak some English. Dale liked me from the beginning and was patient with me. He doesn't speak good Spanish, but between what he speaks and what little English I knew at the time, we both found better ways to talk. 'Communicate' is the word that is better. I learned quickly."

He looked at me with a serious demeanor.

"But you, *cabrón,* you're not just a gringo. You have college. You have skills. You are intelligent. I understand why *I* work for Dale, but what about you? I make more money than you and live in a small room. I save and send back to Mexico some of it to help my family. But you, you could have anything, but here you are. You were a Marine. Why are you working with an illegal for barely more than minimum wage?"

"Because of a girl."

"*Aye, chihuahua!*" he said with a laugh.

A string of Spanish came out of him suddenly as if he was cursing at me.

"Samson had Delilah," he moaned. "Dillinger, this mafia guy or whatever he was, had the woman in red." More Spanish phrases were spoken. "Here is this gringo with everything. Everything! But some girl now has his attention, and here he is with me, hauling logs in a lumberyard. You are a waste. A waste! I would give anything to trade places with you, but here I am, stuck like you, but also stuck *with* you, a crazy one. Just who is this girl that ruined your life? She better be worth it."

"Just passing through, Jose. She's worth it for now."

He studied me. "So you're using her? Why?"

"Jose, I'm still backpacking around the world. This is my latest stop."

"Oh, these spoiled brat *putos*," he said with a laugh. Another string of Spanish came out of him.

"Jose," I returned defensively, "it is a luxury, like you say, to live on nothing when you don't have to and make it all around the world. And in my case, I didn't do it from desperation to find a better life. Or, no, actually, that's exactly why I did it. Just a different version of a better life than you had to find. But there's not only the Taj Mahal and the Eiffel Tower and the Vatican and all to see. There are so many people everywhere to learn from. There are all these bucks to pay out to learn something in college. Backpacking and stopping for jobs here and there was just another education, and it got me on a roll about being educated."

"So, you work with an illegal in Tucson for low wages," he countered, unconvinced by any analogy.

"Yeah, now that. To make my way and continue my education. The education is happening here in Tucson right now. And soon I'll use my skills and be a gringo in the land of opportunity to make the money you think I should pursue. Oh, yes, I'll pursue it. But materialism is a trap if you let it be. Being an American is a trap if you let it be."

"Being an illegal with no possessions is a bigger

trap," he countered. "And I want out of that trap. *Sabes, cabrón?*"

"And now I'm here with you. And loving it. I'm not throwing away my future, Jose. It cost money for my education in college. I get paid for working with you. Little as it is, it's still my education I'm working for. It just looks like a trap to you because you're stuck on the outside—for now, anyway. You're smart. You aren't going to be stuck here for long. Neither am I. But for now, for this part of my education, I'm meeting you and also Mary Lou. I won't be doing this much longer, and it is all a luxury, a luxury I can afford. I would be the shallowest man alive to go straight to college, then straight to a plush job to rise high on the ladder. But then never see the Taj Mahal or meet you, Jose. It lets me know more about who I am and who I want to be. *And* who Jose is and why I'm a better person for knowing him. It was my self-confidence that allowed me all this, allowed me to 'ruin' my life, knowing how I could also fail. I love knowing all that. I want to kick failure's ass!"

Jose studied me more, then started shaking his head. "You're different, *hombre*," he said. "And because you are the person you are and content to work with an illegal in a God-forsaken lumberyard, I've met someone like you *and* didn't have to travel around the world to do it. I just had to cross the Arizona border. You're a good man, Kaleb. But we both face the same challenges."

Chapter Eight

I studied the contestant on stage at the karaoke joint, focusing on his demeanor, how he pounded his guitar, and the occasional jerk of one of his legs or hips. Watching all the performers soon caused me fatigue. It was too late to change my style anyway. Just sing the song, I reassured myself. Enjoy the audience, and relate the song.

It was a contest of nobodies. No names given, not even a song title. Just walk out to the microphone on stage, take a deep breath, and begin.

There was a song by Hank Williams called "The Old Log Train." Slow, melodious, and deep. This was my idea of a song to perform. Hank had little formal education, but the depth of his soul came out in his words easily. They called him the Hillbilly Shakespeare. "The Old Log Train" was another of these songs of his. You wanted to live that soulful life. It meant hard work, but it was part of a blend with nature.

Mary Lou, however, had a better idea. She liked the way I did "Lovesick Blues" with the slurred yodels on certain words. Hank wrote one similar in style to it called "Long Gone Lonesome Blues." which also included half yodels to a nice rhythm. The yodels, the beat, and the clever words of lost love got your attention and bullied you with it at the same time, and Hank did both songs marvelously. But it was endearing to use her selection, making my performance feel more like an "us" thing.

"You were wonderful, Kaleb," she said as I returned to my seat beside her toward the back of the audience. "You did it well this afternoon before we came here. But performing it for the first time in front of a crowd is a different story. You had the most applause up to now. We'll see what happens."

Soon the contest was over and all the performers made their way back to the side of the stage to see who won. When they waved me out to reintroduce me, some of the crowd stood up and cheered. A few whistled.

At the end we all were invited onto the stage together as they announced the winner. My name was called out.

"I'm so proud of you, Kaleb," Mary Lou greeted me as we left the auditorium together. She clutched my arm with both of hers, fully embracing it.

"All this made me nervous," I confessed, "but I felt the best. My ego or whatever."

"You *were* the best," she boasted. "That girl, though, that pranced and flirted with the crowd? You never know. To me that was just a gimmick, but you almost lost to a gimmick. It *did* get attention and got almost as much applause as you. But in the end, raw talent got it. Gimmicks beware. I love it!"

"Is your name Kaleb?" a man asked just outside of the exit.

His boldness caused me to stare. I had seen him somewhere before.

"You're the owner of the place next door, aren't you?" Mary Lou asked him.

"Yes," he replied. "Moonshine, if that's what you're talking about. Sounds like bootleg, and we do serve alcohol, but it means moonlight too, and I prefer the name 'Moonshine.' I've never seen you before, Kaleb, but I noticed you last night with your girlfriend here. She shows up now and then in the crowd at my place."

"I'm always entertained," she replied.

"How would you like to be one of our performers at Moonshine?" he asked me, looking directly and pointedly at me. "You've got a good voice and good style, and I liked your song and the way you performed it. If you could come up with ten songs, I'd give you an hour on stage. If the crowd responds well, you can sing two or three nights a week. We can work that out tomorrow, one way or another."

Mary Lou embraced my arm more tightly, as if celebrating.

"We'd love to," she answered on my behalf. "But let us work out the best nights for us. We'll get back to you tomorrow."

"Tomorrow was going to be one of the nights open for you," the owner said. "The singer tomorrow, a solo singer with a guitar like you, is sick and not up to it. He still wants to sing and even needs the money. But I can't allow that. I understand him needing money, but I'm going to lose all my customers if I put up with situations like that."

"I'll sing," I answered, "and you can pay him what you were going to pay me."

The look on Mary Lou's face showed how proud she was of me.

"That sounds good," the man said. "He'll appreciate that. If the crowd responds to you well, I'll throw in a little tip your way besides."

"What time should we show up?" Mary Lou asked

him.

"Eight is when you'll perform. We aren't a bar. We're sort of a half bar and half restaurant. We include tables for some of the adults that like to hang around if they enjoy the music enough, and we serve alcohol at these tables. I need some good performers, so I'm hoping you work out."

I nodded shyly but felt exuberant. Only my wildest dreams could fathom performing for money in front of a crowd. We shook hands as an informal contract.

"We'll work on the ten songs tonight," Mary Lou swore to the restaurant owner.

"We've got to get up early, Mary Lou."

"You know more than ten songs, Kaleb," she said to me as well as to reassure the owner about me. "We'll go over a few tonight to remind you which ones you feel best about. It won't be long. It won't be a rehearsal. Just a few tonight before we go to bed."

The owner seemed pleased.

"Thanks," I said, showing my approval. "Looking forward to it."

He gave a nod in reply.

The evening put me in a good mood. And Mary Lou soon put me in a better one.

Chapter Nine

"Do you get out much, Jose?" I asked the next day at the lumberyard as we unloaded a truck.

"It's a rough town, Kaleb," he replied. "I'm not afraid of rednecks or *pendejos*, but I'm afraid of the border patrol. If I go to some bar, someday I'm going to get into a fight. The cops come, and then I'm deported. Some cheap enchilada place is good enough. Best is just to go straight home after work. Cheaper too. Twice a year Dale lets me go back to Durango with what I've saved. My parents need what little money I give them. That helps them out with my brothers and sisters. Simple life. Desperate life, Kaleb. Dale likes me and uses me on the forklift, and he taught me how to weld. Someday, I'll look for better. But Dale is very good to me and it's safe right now. If I keep getting across the border safely, my life is good. The border patrol here knows about me too. They look the other way to help people like Dale. And they seem to like me. There's always other border patrol agents to worry about, but so far the ones here look the other way. They protect me. However long that lasts."

Illegals we hired on our farm in south Texas had similar stories. We always had to worry about the border patrol raiding our fields. They knew that we and other farmers needed this cheap help, but they had a job to do. Often times, a border patrol plane would fly over our area checking the fields for work gangs. Not long

53

afterwards a border patrol van would appear and check everyone. We always had a few legals to show them after we hid the illegals. A strong border is needed. The border patrol is good for that, but we needed the illegal workers and some of them we befriended. Enough illegals got through our immigration system that it helped us out for cheap unskilled labor, and helped those lucky enough to make it here to find work, though illegally. Yet if we didn't protect ourselves with help from the border patrol, we knew we would soon feel invaded. Life was complex, and the situation in those years was just another example of that. This complexity appealed to me even at a young age. It made me think through every aspect of life while growing up. My upbringing, as such, spurred my wanting to see the world, as happened years later.

"Does the border patrol come to Dale's lumberyard?" I asked Jose further.

He shook his head. "I've been working here for two years and feel safe. But at risk. It's a simple life. That's good. It's best to save my money anyway."

Few, if any, of the illegals we hired back home, or the ones any of the farmers back home hired, knew English. But Jose, after only two years here, spoke English so well without even a strong accent. That our hands on the farm did not speak English made it harder to get very close to them. It was easy to like them, but we never bonded that much. There was already a cultural divide, an economic divide, and a racial divide. There was much hard manual labor for us on the farm, but especially for the hired farm workers. We were the managers, the overseers. Jose now was filling in some of the gaps for me about this hierarchy. He was special, but still, it got through to me what the life of an illegal was truly like. All this now seemed like a continuation of my going around the world, experiencing in-depth streetwise lessons firsthand.

"I joined the Marine Corps in 1970," I said to Mary Lou that night as we lay in bed before dozing off. "In the middle of my senior year in college. Had my senior ring and was a part of the PLC program of the Marine Corps. PLC stands for Platoon Leaders Class. The Marines didn't have ROTC in those days. If we wanted to work towards a Marine commission while in college, we joined the PLC program. They had meetings to acquaint us with the Marine Corps. We studied some history, did some physical training, and got hands-on officers training in a boot camp environment in Quantico, Virginia at a Marine base. This boot camp for officer candidates was several weeks in the summertime, between college terms. Usually after the junior year. I joined this program my senior year and looked forward to the training at Quantico the next summer. But then, in the fall of 1969, President Nixon and his Secretary of State Henry Kissinger were seeking peace plans with the North Vietnamese. So if I was going to Vietnam, now was the time."

"You *wanted* to go to Vietnam?" Mary Lou asked in amazement.

"Want is a big word," I replied. "Mostly I felt obliged. I was sick of my generation already, and sick of anti-war movements. At first, some of the anti-war stuff made sense and made me think. The land of opportunity, the give-me-your-tired-your-poor place, America was the free world's bastion. Free thinkers. History showed how we tried to appease Hitler, but now my generation not only wanted to appease the Communists, guys like

Mao and Stalin and Castro, but sympathized with Communism itself. But Communism was not only a bad economic system, it was often totalitarian. Suddenly, to my 'enlightened' generation—Ha!—America and the military did nothing right, or humane, while Ho Chi Minh was saving the world from aggression. There were even some decent arguments for a while about some of this and whether or not we belonged in Vietnam. But then all you ever heard was 'us bad, them good.' Much of my generation decided that every reason to fight the Communists, especially North Vietnam, was suspicious or more likely evil. To them the argument about the domino theory was pure hogwash. I knew there was more to the Communists being in Vietnam than the domino theory, for sure. I agreed with that part. That it wasn't the overriding issue about the Vietnam War."

"What's the domino theory?" she asked. "I've heard of it but didn't fully grasp what they were talking about."

"If you stand dominoes up on a table or on the floor in a line width-wise and knock over the first one, every domino beyond that first one gets knocked down too, in the whole line. So, because of World War II, when Hitler was allowed to take over one country after another for his version of justice, many Americans were leery of appeasing the Communists later on. And so many countries were bullied by Communist neighbors. We had fear of passively sitting there and letting the Communists take over other countries one by one similar to the way Hitler took over much of Europe as we appeased him. The Korean War was fought over that, and then Vietnam. We watched Stalin take over and bully much of eastern Europe. Then China became Communist and that made the fear even more pronounced concerning Asia.

Communism becoming a world threat meant we could be stuck with being an island of democracy, just America alone someday, or worse."

Mary Lou nodded her head as if she understood.

"We were getting paranoid about Communist takeovers because of it. We saw the Russians develop Sputnik, then saw them encroach just ninety miles off our shores in Cuba, with sympathy for that from many third-world countries, especially in places where there had been colonialization by European powers. So it is good to notice all these elements and sides and to want to have answers about it."

Mary Lou nodded more. I loved how attentive she was and so eager to learn. It made me think her lack of education to this point was due to a hard and demanding life rather than lack of awareness or curiosity. It made me feel important, to have her listening so intently to me.

"Go on about the domino theory, then," she prodded.

"As we watched one country after another succumb to Communism, or at least be threatened directly by it, we got paranoid, like I said. When these arguments against the Vietnam War were espoused, it became thought-provoking about the world situation around us. Maybe our fears were indeed paranoia. And so, hmm, maybe we, the masses, let ourselves get brainwashed by hard-core militarists. Or the ultra-right-wing John Birch Society and their ilk. I didn't really believe this was the case, not on a massive scale anyway, but I still wanted to know more to decide better. But so much of my anti-war generation railed against our racist society, or the military-industrial complex, or paranoia over the domino theory. Good causes to consider, and there was something worthy about each argument. Except suddenly much of my generation was burning the flag, carrying around and even quoting Mao's little red book, et cetera. These anti-warriors didn't just sound like a different side now, to me, but more like they were getting brainwashed by this other side. Suddenly the domino theory was totally hogwash to them. A lot of people for the war in Vietnam did believe the domino theory to be the dominant element happening. That evil Communists, if left unchecked, would be free to take over and manipulate everyone's lives with evil. But then things got oversimplified by the anti-war crowd that the domino theory was total hogwash. Except I knew it wasn't either/or. The domino theory wasn't just suddenly worthless just because we saw there was more to global politics than that. Meaning, it seemed to me, we were still made up of simpletons. We still had so little perspective. Everything was still so black-and-white to so many. The naïve masses. We had more sides now to choose to be a goon about, really, rather than to have perspective about. People saw little to learn from any of the arguments except to choose sides and then live in their own fortress of virtue and correctness about it."

"Oh, these wonderful talks with you, Kaleb," she said as she stroked my cheek. "You're so interesting."

"Yeah, well," I replied. "It sounds pretty good sometimes, but I can never explain away how President Johnson, a fellow Texan, used the Gulf of Tonkin affair to try to instigate getting us into war. All so he could look strong against the Republican presidential candidate, Barry Goldwater. Goldwater was a 'hawk' and seemed to be scoring some points for squaring off against Communists. Even if we should have done something to stand up to aggressive Communism, look what happened when our government manipulated and plotted to get us into the war just to look macho, like in the Gulf of Tonkin in North Vietnam waters to appease the hawks. Then they worked to keep us out of war behind the scenes because they saw the problems created from war. LBJ didn't want to get stuck with a war they seemed to want to create. War is a loser even if you win it. How do you rectify any of the things our government did back in the sixties? I didn't want to sympathize with any of it, but I joined the Marines anyway. The war was going on. Mao sucked. Ho Chi Minh sucked. Communism sucked. The domino theory had a lot of credence, except there we were, doing whatever we could to start a war, sometimes to win an election, but then trying not to get into the same war at other times so we wouldn't have to deal with horror and pain of war. We really could be bad guys. No hiding from that. One can go along with so many of the anti-war arguments in spite of the evil and the threat of Communism. And in spite of much legitimacy in the domino theory. So, with the war raging, when push came to shove, I joined. Damn well joined. And even now still believe in the war for the reasons I do. I'm not sure at all that we should have been there, though, simply because of the way it was handled and the way we maneuvered to get us into the war and then the way so much of the war was conducted. But I did join from love of country while my country was under attack by so much of my generation. It became a political statement for me to join. Love for country and for our ideals, in spite of our evils, and we had a lot to fight for in spite of the Gulf of Tonkin mindset that got us into it. Communism really was on the move. I wanted to do something about it."

"You make me want to go to college, Kaleb. Yes, I'm going now, but I mean *really* go. Really hear things and learn to think. I've been just surviving up to now. I've been going to college more as a way to find a better job than to be a more complete person. There are trade schools if all I want is a good skill. The more complete person is beginning to matter to me."

"Good," I replied, smiling warmly at her. "Good. Education is so underrated. Books are so underrated. More education will help keep a Vietnam from happening again. But only with perspective. We were so naïve. We still are so naïve, patriots and flag-burners alike. We're so naïve. We all have so much growing up to do to handle both sides of any argument. I've been around the world, but I haven't a clue yet what I've learned by doing that, except that I'm different now. We'll just have to see where all this leads."

"But you didn't just learn from a book, Kaleb. You've been out in the world."

"And those that hate books and school want to believe experience is the only teacher. It may be the best teacher, but books open up so many worlds and lay them right at our feet, right in our living room or classroom. I love all forms of education."

"That is so," she said with a sigh. "You know more than anyone I've ever met and you're only thirty. Books and the road of hard knocks taught you so much."

"You have to want to learn," I answered. "You have to love knowledge."

Chapter Ten

This was to be my debut. My introduction to Tucson as a professional singer. Except the money for it wasn't going to me.

The owner was to supply an acoustic that had an electrical outlet, but I brought my new guitar along for moral support and to find my key with the electric one I would use.

I glanced at my guitar nervously several times on the walk, to reassure myself. Hank did it before me. Johnny Cash and Elvis did it before me. Merle Haggard started off in prison and he ended up all right. Now it was my turn.

Entering the alcohol-abundant establishment made me want to gag. How could people live this way? Whiffs of food and beer were mixed with strong body odors.

I went to the stage area and hoped to be noticed. If no one recognized me, maybe my guitar was a hint. Soon, the owner appeared from a room at the far side.

"You're a bit early, Kaleb. Good. I'll show you around a bit."

He pointed out his office, the toilets, a storage room, the kitchen, and then the side entrance to the stage area. This made me feel more at home.

"A girl's going on before you," he informed me. "That'll warm up the mostly male crowd. She won't be long. A few numbers to get people's minds off of whatever it is they came here to forget. She's been here several times and really charms them. It'll make it easier on you. They'll hate you for not being her, but she'll have their minds away from the bad day they probably just had."

I barely spoke the entire time he showed me around. My focus was on making the crowd happy with my singing. That's if my voice didn't quiver from my nervousness.

When would Mary Lou arrive? She would make me feel more at ease. And she would be here for me so I could make her proud.

"Good luck, Kaleb," I heard her voice say from behind me near the stage.

"Where did you come from, Mary Lou?"

"There's a side entrance," she answered. "I just came from the restaurant and that was closer than their main entrance. They let me off early to come see you. They are happy for you even though they don't know you. We were so busy tonight, but they knew this was important to you. To me, yes, but because of you."

My broad smile was followed by an exaggerated exhale.

"You okay?" she asked. "You gonna make it?"

A nod of assurance was my reply.

"You can sit with me," the owner said to Mary Lou. "You'll like the girl that's going to perform before him. But Kaleb needs to go backstage now. Someone will set up the guitar we have for him. He'll probably want to check out the chords on a couple of songs to make sure it's tuned right for him."

Shifting his gaze to me, the owner continued.

"You tuned your guitar with the electrical tuner I

lent you, so you'll be okay. The electric guitar uses the same tuner. So you'll be in the same key because of it."

"I'll be better if I check all that out." My glance went at the owner, then at Mary Lou.

"You'll be great," she encouraged.

With a serious demeanor, she made ready to lean towards me, but then held back.

"I'm here, Kaleb."

My smile assured both of us. Roll over Beethoven. And tell Tchaikovsky while you're damn at it.

The girl singer clutched her guitar while standing at the side of the stage behind a curtain, waiting to go on. She was petite, but stood with a confident stature as if she owned the place. She looked my way and gave a slight smile before looking back out at the crowd. Maybe her performance would give me clues about what songs the crowd liked.

Soon the owner gave a nod to the girl, and she stepped briskly out to the front of the stage. The man who had handed my guitar to me earlier went before her with a microphone and a stool. A stool the girl ignored. The same guy clicked some button before blowing into the microphone to test the volume before looping the cord around her neck.

"Good evening," she greeted the crowd. "I'm your charmer for the next few minutes. You're a nice-sized crowd. Hope I'm the reason you're here," she said while strumming an intro on her guitar. The crowd immediately and politely applauded. I swooned at her sweet voice and how she backed herself on the guitar so nicely. More than rhythm, she supplied catchy riffs to complement her songs, but I was mostly interested in her song selections and the crowd reactions to them. Ballads, both country and folk, were her repertoire. That sounded good to me.

Memories reminded me of the first time I saw Charley Pride on television. He was a rising black star in country music, but it was his style that caught my eye. He walked energetically to the microphone on whatever show it was, all the while not smiling, very serious, as if he was a man on a mission. He went emphatically at his singing from there. They were catchy songs, but mostly it was the straightforward way he sang them that attracted me. He was totally no-nonsense, and it mesmerized me. I decided to do that. Just get out to the microphone and do my business.

Even with the girl's performance before me, I wasn't completely sure what the crowd wanted or expected. But I was going to deliver, and I was not going to dramatize while doing it. No swiveling of my legs or hips. Just the song and me, accompanied by my guitar.

The crowd liked all my songs. Ballads like "Detroit City" and "Sweet Dreams" worked, as did macho songs like "Understand Your Man," as well as patriotic story songs like "The Ballad of New Orleans."

Every last song worked. Much of the crowd held up lit cigarette lighters to me while I sang. Public smoking was illegal in Arizona for the last several years and I wondered why they had them, but they sure came in handy for my performance on my first night.

"You hooked them," the owner said to me as I departed the stage. He had come out of the crowd to greet me. Mary Lou was with him. Her smile was wide and bright as she hugged me tightly before kissing me. She radiated pride for me.

"Listen, there's not too many openings for you right

now," the owner said further, "but we're going to check this out. We're going to see if you're a one-performance wonder or not. We'll fit you in and see what happens next. I'll let you know. My original singer whose place you took still has a cold, so you should get to replace him at least once more. Be patient with me. I'll get you back on stage soon."

We shook hands. My broad grin did all my talking. Mary Lou squeezed my arm tightly as we walked back to our apartment after leaving the restaurant.

It was impossible for me to not envision stardom. To not make fantasies of being the next Hank Williams. Would I ever feel this way again? It was best to enjoy things while I had the chance and let the future take care of itself.

Mary Lou was the perfect distraction for my ego. Her dreams for me seemed even bigger fantasies than my own. And those dreams followed us into our sleep.

Chapter Eleven

Dale is normally courteous, though in a gruff manner, as he grumbles out his morning greetings when we show up for work each day. This time he walked straight to me looking quizzical and cynical.

"I have a friend," he began. "He went to a place near here called Moonshine. There was some new singer from Texas. It turns out it was you."

He waited for me to respond. I simply shrugged.

"How long you been doing this?" he asked.

"A couple of weeks," I replied.

"You seem to be up to it. It hasn't slowed your workload here. That I can tell. But people from Texas can't sing."

"There's more country singers from Texas than anywhere else."

"But who listens to that crap?" he returned.

"Almost everybody. And on top of that, Buddy Holly was from Texas, *and* the Winters brothers, *and* Janis Joplin. And a ton of people in pop and country music you never bothered to care about."

"You've got an answer for everything," he said with a sneer.

"That's what they're there for," I came back.

"This is what I mean," he spit out. "You don't show much respect."

"I respect you, Dale, but I also react to you. I'm

doing my job. You're doing yours."

"What's that supposed to mean?"

"It means you started off this conversation like I might be intruding on getting things done here because of singing a couple of nights a week at a bar. Then you wondered how someone like me could be a singer."

"Why is a college-educated guy like yourself working low wages unloading wood?"

"You don't have to know, Dale. But thank you for the job."

"I heard you're pretty good," Dale added, almost smiling. "My friend checked you out and was impressed. The crowd seems to get into you. How long you going to hang around here?"

"It's good here. I'm a farm boy. Not that I don't want better in my life, but I've been doing this kind of work forever. It's good here and I like you and Jose."

Dale squinted. It made me wonder if it shocked him that someone out there liked him. I wondered if anyone that ever worked for him liked him. Besides Jose and me.

"Me and my old lady might come in some night," Dale said, still with his half-smile. "Except we don't like country music."

"Well, you're welcome, for sure."

Jose was nearby, sweeping, close by a pile of logs. When Dale left, he walked over to me with a grin on his face.

"Boss man seems to like you," he commented. "He never talks politely to an employee. He even smiled at you. I think."

"I've dealt with worse than him," I replied.

"You're still crazy to put up with a job some illegal can get, but you've got style. You take life as it comes.

You're a survivor. Like me."

"That's the biggest compliment anyone's ever given me, Jose."

"To be a survivor isn't a compliment for you, Gringo. You've got it made."

"But you said something else," I answered. "You used the phrase, *I'm like you*."

Jose studied me and broadened his smile.

"You're not like anybody, Gringo. You're like out of some folk story."

This scared me. To be happy with my life in Tucson was disorienting. First my life with Mary Lou, then Jose, now the bossman *patrón*. It made me afraid of getting too settled. To be from Texas suited me fine. But here I was now. Happy. There wasn't room inside for being from both a Tucson and a Texas. But enjoying myself in my new circumstances felt good. I'd enjoyed myself in a lot of places as long as it was just passing through. It felt too much like home all of a sudden, now, instead of just passing through. Most other places were foreign countries. Even when I flirted with staying in them, it wasn't a serious thought. But now, staying with Mary Lou, Jose, and even Dale, made me feel more snug than sure of myself. Tucson was a nice enough place, even if it included making a living doing manual labor and living in a shoebox.

"I can't watch you sing tonight, Kaleb," Mary Lou told me upon my arrival home. "It was so busy at the restaurant last night, and they expect more of the same tonight. More tourists or truck drivers or whoever, and they need all hands on deck. I can't let them down."

"I'll manage, but it'll take some of the wind out of my sails."

"You'll be okay. Just picture me slaving away and wanting to be with you. One for the Gipper, you know."

"Maybe it'll make my tearjerkers sadder. Perhaps I should thank you."

"Ha, ha," she said with a giggle. "We'll have to get used to it, you know. I'll be needed a lot at the restaurant."

That night I felt a sting, with Mary Lou gone. It made the tearjerkers seem real, but from frustration more than true heartache. We had seemed to share my pain together when I sang them before, at our apartment. They were more endearing there. Sharing loneliness together was more togetherness than lonely.

I beat her home that night, and by the time she got home I'd already showered, and was ready for bed.

"I'm so sorry, Kaleb," she said anxiously as she came in from work. "But at least the tips were great, overall, and I sure need the money. So I'm hoping you did well, but I am glad for the extra work."

"I sang more upbeat songs tonight. To get myself out of the dumps. I wasn't really in the dumps, but maybe a little. Anyway, the upbeat ones got me more applause. I love the ballads too much to not sing them, but maybe I'll include more upbeat ones now."

"There," she said as she gave me a hug. "It worked out for both of us. That's what survivors do. We're working-class stock. All this makes us strong."

"Don't get me happy," I lectured her. "I need you there. Ah, and guess what else?"

"What else, then?" she asked with a tease.

"I introduced a new song tonight. A ballad, even."

"Which one? You've got a lot of new ones you could use."

"Yeah, but this is the best."

She waited patiently for my answer.

" 'Take My Hand for a While.' " I snickered. "There, you missed 'Take My Hand for a While.' You're not so hot now, even with your tips."

"Oh, Kaleb, that's not fair. You did that on purpose! To teach me a lesson! It's almost cruel. How could you sing that without me?"

"You never showed up, and I needed that song. It reenergized me. The crowd loved it even though it was a tearjerker."

"I'm sure they did. But you weren't sure about the guitar part. Sometimes you miss a chord. What made you decide to try it? I'm glad you survived."

"Well, I didn't miss any chords. And they loved it. I'm going to sing it regularly."

"Okay, that way I'll get to hear you. I might have to work late more often now. I'd buy you a beer in celebration, but I'm exhausted. I'm not even going to shower, though I'm all sweaty. Good luck with that."

"Working-class heroes turn me on. You know that."

Chapter Twelve

"That's too lonely, Kaleb," Mary Lou instructed me. "It's a nice song, though. Just so sad. But you did it well. Still, it's so tragic maybe you shouldn't sing it. Not sure which is worse, the first verse or the last. The two middle verses are just sad. But the first verse breaks my heart, and then the last one just makes me want to curl up in the fetal position and try to survive."

"Hank Williams wrote some really sad songs," I commented sullenly. "That song is probably his saddest. It may be the saddest song I've ever heard."

"Sing the last verse again," she beckoned. "I'll be braver this time. It was beautiful. Tragic, but beautiful."

Emotions struggled inside her throughout the song. At the end she began to sing with me.

"You know," I said, "you have a pretty voice. Why haven't you sung to me before? You know some of the songs I sing now. Why is this the first time you sang with me?"

She shrugged.

"To hear you sing better," she answered. "We were getting to know each other, and then it turned out you could sing. Then it turned out you got a job as a singer. There was never the urge to sing for me." She gave another shrug with her shoulders. "Until now."

"And you had my key. At least for that one verse."

"It was a bit low for me, but close enough. You're a

tenor. Not far from my key."

"Well, you did it great."

"Great, he says. Suddenly I'm great."

"I always wanted to have a girl sing with me. Let's do it together. Let's work out an arrangement of this song."

"What?" she asked with a chuckle. "What are you thinking in that mind of yours? I never sing except now and then with the radio, or in church with the congregation. Don't start getting ideas."

"Ideas about what?" I teased. "I'm only saying let's sing this song together since you already sang part of it with me and it was good."

"What are the words?" she countered.

"You sort of know them. And they're easy."

"Is this a bonding moment?" she asked.

"It's a good moment, for sure. The two of us singing together since we both like this song so much. So let's find your key, your comfort zone."

After finding the progression that worked best for us, we expanded on the song. A broad smile oozed onto her face after we finished.

"You were wonderful," I told her.

She blushed.

"Thanks, Kaleb. It brings back wonderful memories of my father. I was ready to cry at times, just now, 'cause it was so fulfilling, like just being a little girl sitting on his lap while he sang. He seemed to like me there on his lap, but it wasn't like he was singing *to* me... He was sharing *with* me."

"We're falling in love," I said softly, staring at her, starry-eyed.

"Oh, Kaleb, don't. I'll start crying. Drop this."

"Listen, Mary Lou. Come to Moonshine tonight. If there's a way to keep from working late, do so. Come to me at Moonshine. If you could make it even the last fifteen minutes of my hour there, I want you to sing this song with me. I won't sing it if you're not there. It is too morbid a song for a restless crowd. It's more than just sad. It's melodious with haunting words. If an angel like you sings it with me, though, it'll fly. Emmy Lou Harris sang this song angelically and made it almost sound like a lullaby, except for such morbid words. The words didn't sting when she sang them. They made you want to comfort her. Do it, Mary Lou! We'll explain to the audience this is your debut, just in case you're so nervous you want to die. They'll be pulling for you. I'll do the singing, and you'll just sing with me. And wait until the second verse to come in—so I do the first verse, you with me on the second, me the third, and then you and me on the fourth. You can handle that. You can! Practice to yourself while I'm at work. When you are beyond stage fright, meaning later on, if there is a later on, maybe management will let you duet with me. But tonight just sing this one song with me. Come in on the second verse and sing along with me. Later on, someday, I'll have you sing the second by yourself. You can handle that. Then the fourth together with me again. I'll do the first and third solo."

"Ah, Kaleb, no… Why did I have to sing that fourth verse with you just now? Ah!"

"So, you'll do it, then?"

She nodded her head enthusiastically.

"We'll tell management this is your debut, and it's just for this one song, with me the lead singer. The crowd will be sympathetic. Worst case scenario, it'll be over and everyone recovers. Maybe."

"Oh, such encouragement," she said while punching me gently at my upper arm.

"You'll do fine. Just join in. Let's practice now. Just this one song, and then it's back to work. Boy-girl arrangements are wonderful, you know. Groups like Peter, Paul and Mary, the New Christy Minstrels, Paul and Paula. They're from the sixties, when I was growing up. Even Glen Campbell and Bobbie Gentry. It's harmonious, and not just the singing. The *spirit* of it. This will work, promise."

She started shaking her head no. "Okay," she finally said after a small pause. "I'd even love it. If you think so much of my singing, I'll give myself benefit of the doubt. I'll manage somehow."

New fervor engulfed me upon returning to Moonshine to sing that night. My one angst, however—would Mary Lou show up?

Halfway through my performance, right in the middle of a Johnny Horton ballad, she walked through the door and made her way toward the stage area. She was early. Either her restaurant duties were manageable or her boss took pity at the thought of costing her a debut as my singing partner.

Instead of coming to the side of the stage, she sat on an empty chair borrowed from a table, to be by herself while watching me. A simple nod by me was her cue to come on stage.

"You were wonderful," I told her immediately after the song. "The crowd was standing and cheering. You knew the words. We practiced a lot, but the words are simple and—Pow! We did this! This was your debut and you didn't panic. The crowd was more than supportive for a shy debut singer. They loved us! They loved *you*, Mary Lou. Dramatic kisses your way, right here and now, girl. This is going to work!"

Chapter Thirteen

"I've got to meet this girl, Kaleb," Jose said to me as we moved a beam together to another part of the lumberyard. "She gets you out of a murder rap, puts you up in her apartment, helps you find a job, then gets you a standing ovation when she sings with you in your starring moment. If you don't marry her, you are a *puto*, Kaleb. And I hope you know what that means."

"Thanks anyway, Jose. I love your mother too. I'm not ready to get married. Neither one of us are. But more and more it's getting to be a wonderful thought."

I understood just enough of what Jose was slurring my way in Spanish to know he was still on my case about Mary Lou and our civil status together.

"When do you go to this Moonshine place again?" Jose asked me.

"Yo," we heard as we placed the beam down in one of the shelters.

"Daddy's calling us," Jose said with a laugh as Dale approached.

"What are you two up to?" he asked when he reached us in the shelter. "I told both of you to put that beam on that truck out front. It was even closer from where you picked it up than it is from here. Now you've got to take it back, except keep going until you get to the truck. Then, when it's loaded, there's a bunch of boards to load onto the truck too. You think you can get all this straight now? We need it at the warehouse this afternoon. You'll have to work late if you don't hustle now."

Dale looked at me.

"It would be a shame for you to miss your singing job at Moonshine," he said with a grin. "A friend of mine from church told me about this Texas guy and this waitress girl singing and people going crazy over it. I'm going to have to check this out for myself finally. I'll bring the wife. Tonight, right? Don't you go on tonight?" I gave a nod. Dale then looked at Jose. "Did you know he was a singer?"

"He's telling me all of this now," Jose replied. "And how this girl keeps doing all these things for him while he is one broke and stupid *cabrón*. I'm going to hear him sing just to meet her and talk her into marrying me. I'm better looking than Kaleb and, it turns out, twice as smart too."

"You want to go, then, Jose? Me and the missus are going to check it out tonight. You don't have a car. I'll pick you up and you can go with us."

"*Muchas gracias*, Dale."

Dale was a guy who was hard to like until you saw what a good man he was underneath the rough exterior. He had a rough edge he'd probably developed by being a *patrón* most of his adult life. The thought of him and Jose being in the crowd warmed me.

There was a second song to include Mary Lou now. "Cotton Fields" was fairly well known, or at least known of. Mary Lou knew of it too, and since Credence Clearwater Revival had sung it a few years before, using only the first verse and refrain over and over, I chose to do it their way. The second verse of the song was good too, but with Mary Lou being new to singing, the simpler the better. For now.

And simple worked. She was perfect. Dale and Jose greeted us as we made our way from the stage after our performance. They could not hold back their enthusiasm.

"Who can believe this guy?" Jose cried out happily as he rushed over to me to shake my hand. "*Aye, Chihuahua, hombre!*" And he went into several other Spanish exclamations as he put his arm around me in celebration. When he looked at Mary Lou next, he added, "and this is the girl he tells me about. Mary Lou is your name. It's so good to finally meet you!" He seemingly wanted to hug her, but held back. "Why is this the first time for me to see you here? But who could know he would be so good! That his singing partner was an angel, and even better than our *compadre* here."

"Everything Jose said," Dale exclaimed as he shook my hand while allowing a half smile to appear on his face. "That was really good. My wife greatly enjoyed it also. She's going to tell her friends and her club members. She's already talking about hiring you two for parties and outings they have. But you've got to give Mary Lou more singing time."

"She'll be my full partner soon," I explained. "We've only just formed as a duet, so I'm breaking her in slowly."

"You've still got to show up for work tomorrow," Dale said in exaggerated gruffness. It was part of his approval of me. "And I expect just as much work from you, also. You better go straight home and be fresh for tomorrow."

He then looked at Mary Lou.

"Sometimes we need a third helper at the lumberyard, but Jose and Kaleb are stout and able, and they get it done. Even logs sometimes. Fairly large ones. Not tree trunks. But fair-sized logs."

He looked at me with approval, and then at Jose.

"Well, Jose," he said, "the wife is waiting for us to get to the car and go home. Mary Lou has a car for you two, is that right?"

She nodded that she did. "We're going straight home. I have classes early in the morning and need to be alert."

"You're a student?" Dale mused. "Kaleb said you were a waitress."

"I'm a student working her way through college," she explained.

"Is that so? Let me talk to my dad. He loves stories like yours, Mary Lou. Unless you prefer to stay a waitress, maybe we can find you work in our office. Come by and talk to our office foreman and tell her what you can do. Office skills or whatever. We'll find a place for you. Unless your tips are so large at the restaurant that you don't want to leave it. Anyway, come by. Let's see if we can find something mutually beneficial."

"Why, thank you, Dale. Your daughter, the office foreman, is a friend of mine. We were talking last week and suddenly previous conversations about our circumstances made sense. I'm sorry. I shouldn't be calling you Dale. We just met."

"That's my name," he answered. "If you want me to answer you, that's what you call me."

"That's so kind of you."

"Oh, man," Jose groaned with exaggeration. "All this getting along. Hey, boss, you're making me sick inside with all this sweetness and praise."

"You'll get over it, Jose. Tomorrow I'll ride your

butt even harder."

"*Bueno*," he said with a laugh. "I'm feeling better already."

Chapter Fourteen

"I'm getting big tips lately," Mary Lou said with a broad smile on her face. This worked as her greeting to me after arriving home from Hank's.

"So," I returned, "that means we're getting a bigger apartment?"

"That means I can save a dime or two, finally. There's never anything to spare if something goes wrong. And there's no compensation for me if I get hurt, unless it's on the job. So spending more is still a luxury. Maybe I can save some now and then, instead. You helping with the rent is good too."

"So, Dale asked me if you were going to take him up on his job offer. It would be steady work, with set hours."

"No tips, though," she replied, staring at me in thought. "I'll think about it. You're giving me more exposure singing now. These tips I'm getting at Hank's are because of my singing. Some of the tippers tell me that anyway."

"But your salary is still miniscule. And you have no insurance. He'd give you medical insurance and Social Security. It's standard for fulltime employees."

"What does he have in mind? I don't have any secretarial skills. Maybe his daughter can find out for me, since she's my friend. I wouldn't be any good in the lumberyard with you and Jose, that's for sure."

"He probably sees you as a receptionist. His daughter there talks to him about you. He has his office and he greets customers that come in. When he's out, he uses her for this. You'll be a receptionist and probably file things away and run errands. No idea. You'd have to work around your classes, but he'll be sympathetic to that. You can work late sometimes, or on Saturday a bit."

"A girl Friday," she mused.

"You'd have insurance and also have set hours and permanency," I repeated to her in order to drill it in. "That's a pretty good tradeoff for lack of tips."

"Yeah," she said enthusiastically. "Yeah. That's a good tradeoff. You'll be leaving for work soon. I'll drive you there and then talk to him and say I'm ready. I'll tell Hank's this afternoon that I'm leaving as soon as they get a new waitress. You and I can flirt with one another some at the lumberyard. Maybe have lunch together. I'll fix lunch for both of us. This is looking up, Kaleb. There's a happy feeling inside just thinking about it. Before, I was just surviving. Now I'm happy."

"See, I'm worth having around. Not just you doing all the happiness work here. I'm making my way now with you."

"We're getting domesticated, aren't we?" She gave me a wink.

"It's nice. I was going to retire my travelling gear when I got back to Texas. Now, I'm thinking of not going back at all."

"I'm glad you said that, Kaleb, but I don't want to think about it. We're living one day at a time and each day gets better. Let's just do that. What would you do in Texas, by the way, if you did go back? You have a degree and you're ready to settle down. But was there something specifically on your mind if you did get back to Texas?"

"Nothing," I answered. "Maybe get a master's degree. That would make me more skilled and buy me some time, too, to sort my life out. Nashville crossed my mind, working bars, hoping to get discovered as a singer eventually. But that's too much like not settling down. More of the same doesn't cut it anymore." I stared at her pointedly. "I'm ready to settle down now, because of you."

"You thought about a master's, you say. You were a good student, then. I'm barely making it. I'm on probation and I'm only in junior college. No four-year institution is going to put up with the likes of me."

"Well, Dale hired you, and soon you'll be a front office girl for him. He'll even give you time to go to classes since you're only taking a few. I'll whip you into shape. You'll get your grades up. Do you have a major? Probably not, from the sound of it."

She shook her head. "School is so heavy on me," she said with a grimace.

"That's ninety percent of your bad grades right there. Education is wonderful. Knowledge is power. I'll be your guide."

"Oh, my God." She sighed. "I got your attention by rescuing you. But you were really sent here to rescue me."

"That's how it works."

"As long as it works," she replied.

But you don't just turn someone's mindset around. I was aware of that from personal experience. There was more to do than just show her the ropes of how to study or give her pep talks. Somehow I had to get it through to her the real power of knowledge, the broadened horizons gained from it, the enduring qualities of a challenged mind. Learning wasn't just memorizing formulas or dates or places. Knowledge was soul food. I needed some help from Pavlov along the way. Conditioned response from improved study habits. The stimuli coming from me. With love and care, she would appreciate education and knowledge someday.

"Thomas Edison," I told her one night as we studied algebra, the subject she hated most, "went through hundreds of substances to see which conducted electricity the best. Now we have the light bulb."

"Yeah, but I'm no Thomas Edison, Kaleb. Don't even start with that. I'm a waitress."

"And you're going to stay one if you don't relate to more of the world. There's more to life than the eastern half of Tucson, Arizona. Right near you is the Painted Desert and the Petrified Forest. If you go very far from here and tell someone you're from Arizona, they are going to think you live among the cactus and sand dunes. They might not even know the Grand Canyon is nearby. Arizona has the most national monuments of any state. People are flocking here for the sunshine when it used to be thought of as just plain hot and suffocating. You have to believe in yourself, Mary Lou, and do so not by pretending you're special, but by understanding all you have to offer—and you do, Mary Lou. You have so much to offer, and I'm going to prove it to you by showing you."

She looked at me, squinting, while pondering all I said. "What do I have to offer?" she finally asked.

"That's where we start. You have to start understanding who you are. You didn't even know you could sing until I brought it up to you. And then ovations from the crowds convinced you. You saved my life. But that's not why I fell in love with you. That just got my attention. Math is boring until it opens up more of the world to you, when you feel the power of the formulas. And while we're at it, we'll find out more about the Declaration of Independence and also our Constitution. You'll see firsthand the path knowledge sets for us. We didn't just defeat the British, Mary Lou, although it was a big deal to beat the major world power back then. We created a country that later helped the British defeat the Nazis."

"You're a special guy, Kaleb, and I appreciate what you're trying to do. But math still frightens me." She turned away, then looked back at me once again. "But yeah," she confirmed, "math doesn't suck as much as it did five minutes ago. And if it helps me pay my bills, then all the better. Math is real. And will soon be a blessing to me more than it is a chore. I'm no Einstein, but something's bigger inside now."

"Math is here to serve us," I stated, "not to torture us."

She let out a giggle. "Boy, who thought I'd have to change my attitude. It is time to grow up about some things, for sure, but this beats the cake."

"I don't really cherish math all that much myself," I stated. "But there's a need for education, and the awareness of that fact makes me pursue things more."

"Stiff upper lip and all," she said.

"Beyond that. When you appreciate things for their value, it lures you rather than threatens you."

She nodded her head, thought a bit, then nodded again.

"When you're working to feed your family," I

lectured her, "it seems more like a blessing than it does work, though you still have to put up with it."

"There," she blurted out. "That one. Yes, I'm so grateful to have a job. There's more blessing than toil in having my job."

"Education opens so many worlds to us, Mary Lou. Blessed ones. Even the parts of education that show the evil in the world. We need to know *about* evil in the world. Not so we *do* evil, but to understand the world. To *overcome* whatever evil we meet in the world."

"Okay, okay, Kaleb. You got it through. Thanks. New perspective here inside me taking shape right in front of our eyes. Sort of. Let me get at it again with my math assignment. I'll need your help, still, and reassurance, but all you said inspires me."

Struggling together helped bring us closer, like being part of a team. We were not just sharing the struggles themselves, but harmonizing life from overcoming those struggles. Our time together now was bonding us even more. The negatives themselves seemed sweet because they were part of the journey we travelled.

"When are you two going to sing together again?" Dale asked us at the lumberyard one day. "Some of my friends want to come see you."

"We sing tonight," I answered him.

"Does she sing more than just a song or two with you now?" he asked.

"We sing fifteen," I replied. "All of them together. The owner likes us. Business has picked up since we started singing together. So, we get fifteen songs now. It lasts over an hour, but it varies a bit from night to night, up to an hour and a half sometimes. That's about the longest we've been on stage. Anyway, she's in on all fifteen with me now. We've got it down."

"It's hard to like country music," Dale confessed. "Not many of my friends like it either. But both me and my wife really like the way you two sing those songs. So you'll have some fans there. We'll shout out to make you look important."

This put a smile on my face. Dale was still gruff with Jose and me, but his affection got through. Tucson was home now. As nice as that was, it also worried me. Texas still had a hold on me, but I was beginning to wonder why.

Chapter Fifteen

"There's a movie out," Mary Lou said to the audience, "Cabaret. 1972, I think it was. It's my favorite movie. Anyway, the theme was 'life is a cabaret' and then it would mix a scene from the day-to-day life of the Liza Minelli character with a song that seemed like it was out of a soundtrack about that part of her life. Well—"

"What she's trying to say," I cut in, "is that Mary Lou has come around. We're a duet now. And this fine establishment—"

"Moonshine, you know," Mary Lou blurted out.

"She's my full partner now at this fine establishment we all love and know as Moonshine. And just as swiftly, the proud owner gave us a whole extra hour to entertain you. And we know you're entertained or you wouldn't be here in droves night after night when we appear. So... Ha! We had to prepare a whole batch of new songs. We knew enough songs to fill the gap easily. But what is the best way to entertain you?"

"Now the part about Cabaret," Mary Lou bellowed. "I'm the only one here that knows this. Not counting Kaleb. He knows because he's at the center of it. Kaleb is from Texas. He was on his way back there, hitchhiking from LA, when he got arrested for murder, right here in Tucson. Just up the road, in fact." She paused with a smirk on her face as she waited for the crowd's reaction. Her announcement got the groans and stares she expected.

"Y'all have to admit," I said with a straight face, "that's worse than when Johnny Rodriguez stole that goat."

A few spurts of laughter came out of the crowd, though most were staring in disbelief while seemingly waiting for further explanation about the murder rap.

"I happened to be waiting tables," Mary Lou explained further, while glaring at the audience, "when this tall hunk of Texan entered and ordered tacos. See, I still remember what he ordered. Then he went over to our jukebox and played a song."

" 'Take My Hand for a While,' " I intervened. "It's still on the jukebox even now, over at Hank's Cowboy Grill. Give it a listen, why don't you?"

"Well, we had a nice chat about the song, how and why we both liked it so much. So how in the hell was I going to forget him after that? Turns out, just outside of town at a truck stop, there was a guy that looked something like my friend Kaleb here, and he was also hitchhiking along I-10. As the truck driver pulled over to let him out, the hitchhiker slit the truck driver's throat and stole his money. And just like in that Lefty Frizell song 'Long Black Veil,' the slayer who ran looked a lot like Kaleb here. I hope Dale, Kaleb's boss at the lumberyard where he works, doesn't fire him after this. I bet you didn't know you hired a guy that had been arrested for murder, did you, Dale?"

"I've hired seedier characters," Dale said, though not many people heard him.

"Well," Mary Lou continued, "suddenly two cop cars pull up at Hank's where I was waiting tables. They had Kaleb in the back seat of one of them. A cop gets out of his car and comes in to ask me if indeed Kaleb had been at the restaurant at the time when the murder occurred. He had me look out the window to identify Kaleb, who had his head sticking out of one of the cop cars. You've got to be kidding me! I thought. Even though I recognized Kaleb and knew he had indeed been in the restaurant at the time described, I still had to think about just what to say, and what if he *was* the murderer somehow, and what if I get him off and there's this murderer alone with me while I'm walking home. But almost right away the full brunt of it all hit me. Poor Kaleb had been arrested for murder that was committed while we were bonding over a song on our jukebox. I was the only one who knew that positively. And only I could get him off."

She paused to let the story she told fully sink in with the crowd.

"Imagine being arrested for murder," she continued forcefully. "In 'Long Black Veil,' the Lefty Frizell character also had an alibi, but it was one who didn't speak up for him. So that song was on my mind when I got Kaleb here off. And, a follow-through to the story—the real murderer was arrested soon after that for another mugging, this one not involving murder. This guy sat in jail for a week before it came out that he was the murderer of that truck driver. So it's at least possible Kaleb would have gotten off anyway, who knows. Yeah, who knows what would have been the outcome if Kaleb had been booked for that murder before the real dude got linked with it."

"And in honor of our *Cabaret* theme tonight," I interrupted with a rather cynical twist, "one of our new songs to lay on you is a Beatles song. You'll recognize it and you'll never let go of what you just heard every time an oldie but goody of 'Run For Your Life' comes on the radio."

The audience howled in laughter. Even Dale managed a laugh. As did his wife, along with Jose going through motions of hysteria.

After the song, I explained another episode that resembled a *Cabaret*-style scene of my life on the road.

"I loved listening to the Depression-era songs of Jimmie Rogers," I said wanting to direct our thoughts from such gore as murder. "The Father of Country Music they called him. Originally from Mississippi, he spent much of his life in the state of Texas. My state. I would listen to him on the radio at times, even though he was long deceased.

"And his songs made me want to experience the life of a bum. Not a railroad bum, as he had been, though I did hop a few freight trains in my backpacking adventures. The one of his that really tugged at me was about a hobo. It is so beautiful, both the melody and the words, that I just had to include it in our expanded list of songs for you and share the imagery of the song before Mary Lou and I sing it for you.

"It fits our *Cabaret* theme in that it is the life I've lived these last couple of years backpacking all around the world. It's been such an experience, with such peace, in so many different cultures and histories, grandeur like you could never imagine and poverty beyond anything we've ever experienced in America. This song followed me in my travels. So much so that I was even grateful to Jimmie Rodgers for opening me up to being a bum.

"I'm skilled and educated and love that America is prosperous. But I'm grateful I've experienced so many other environments and conditions. Linda Ronstadt later sang this song too. Her angelic voice somehow sweetly detracted from the grim but holy-like scene that the song brings to mind with the hope there are freight trains in heaven to ride for eternity. Yes, thank you, Jimmie Rodgers. The hobo is not to scorn. He is to envy."

"If Kaleb had never heard that song," Mary Lou said nostalgically, "we would never have met. That is a lonely, lonely thought for me to ponder and shudder to think. And you would have never met him either."

Chapter Sixteen

"So, *cabrón*," Jose teased me the next day at the lumberyard, "I work on this side of the shed, you the other. I have to keep my eye on you. I had no idea until last night that my life could be in danger at any minute. What will set you off next time? But Dale wants to keep you. He figures he can still kick your ass, but you might come in handy if the Mafia tries to invade the lumberyard."

"Achh!" I groaned. "Right. And you're so funny. Ha."

"It was funny," Jose related. "We could not believe we're hearing this story about this guy arrested for murder. This guy here. *This guy right here among us. Right here in Tucson.* I don't think Dale would have hired you if he had known. I know and he knows you got off. But we know you now. It's easy to believe you are innocent. Especially since they caught the real killer. But someone applies for a job, you don't read on the application, 'arrested for murder in Tucson in 1979.' Who the hell wants to hire someone like that? She had real courage to get you off and then take care of you. They told her the time of the murder and you were there with her then, but still, something inside her was leery, like, 'What if it really was him and I got him off of a murder charge? Am I next?' "

"Well, it wasn't fun getting arrested, I can tell you,"

I affirmed. "The cops kept driving by and eyeballing me while I was at that roadside park. It was dark and I was alone. I thought they must be wondering if I was safe. But instead they were thinking they'd found the murderer. Me!"

"See, *hombre*, this is why I never go out. So many crazies out there. I believe your story, *cabrón.* They let you go on her word even before they found the real murderer. So, they don't want to arrest an innocent man, but they don't want to let a murderer loose, either.

"They had to arrest you just because you looked like the real guy. And Mary Lou didn't know you. She only just met you that day, so she wasn't trying to get a friend off the hook. But imagine if I was an illegal and that happened to me. Oh, they would believe it was me even if they wanted to be fair."

"Sometimes you don't want to get up in the morning," I said, hoping to sound philosophical.

"How long you staying here, Kaleb? You have college. You were a Marine. You've got it made. Why you wasting your time with illegals and murderers? Get back to Texas and start your life. Why are you this *puto* who goes hitchhiking around the world with five pesos in his pocket? I would be doing anything but that. Get your ass back to Texas and start your worthless life, *pendejo.*"

"I like it here, Jose."

"He likes it here." Jose started throwing trash pieces of wood out of the shed area in a crude, pronounced fashion, as if letting off steam. "*I* like it here, Kaleb. *You* don't. You want to be a businessman or a lawyer or something. Not carrying logs off a truck with an illegal." He began throwing more trash pieces while slurring

Spanish curse words in frustration.

"I'm staying a little longer, Jose. It doesn't make sense, I got that. But I'm broke and settled here after all this traveling. I want to think about my life while I'm settled here a bit."

"He wants to think about his life. Achh. You are one crazy *hombre*. What's here for you to think about? Maybe a certain *señorita* is what you think about, eh, *cabrón*?"

I answered with a nod of my head. "She needs me. Now that I'm making some money, I'm helping her pay her rent. It isn't much, but she's putting herself through school. She lives on nothing. Has a beat-up old car. It's paid off, but she can't afford to get it fixed if it breaks down. She doesn't have any credit, either. What little she makes goes for living and school. Both are cheap. But she barely survives. Her mother and sister are nearby and they also don't have anything. Everyone lives day to day without vision. Just surviving and hoping she is smart enough to get into a four-year college and maybe get a job that pays middle class. If I leave now, I'd feel like I'm abandoning her. She saved my life. I even care for her and want to help her, not just money-wise, but help her get some focus and self-confidence, too."

"You going to marry her, *hombre*?"

I shrugged my shoulders.

"He's really thinking about it. *Hombre*, you got your own problems. Don't solve the whole world's problems. You are going to have to solve yours, and they are going to be bigger problems the longer it takes you to get there. Look at you. Working with an illegal in a lumberyard and you're thirty years old? You're going to be doing this when you're fifty if you don't get your ass back to

Texas and use your college smarts."

"I've got some decisions to make real soon," I concurred. "In the meantime, Dale has a lot of work for us to do."

Chapter Seventeen

"Mary Lou, I called home to tell my parents I'm still in Tucson. That I never left after all. So, of course, me working in a lumberyard came up. As did that I'm a singer in a bar. Well, things went downhill from there. They've been trying to get hold of me but didn't know exactly where I was. Last they knew, I was in Los Angeles and heading back to Texas except stuck in Tucson for a while. Well, a month later—"

"A month and a half later, Kaleb," she corrected.

"Anyway, they decided I was either dead or off on some tangent. Again."

"I'll never have a kid like you, Kaleb," she blurted out. "There would never be any sleep. The nightmares and worry would keep me awake. Your parents are chain smokers by now, even if they didn't already smoke before."

"Do you want to hear about the telephone call yet or not?"

She nodded then pursed her lips, preparing for what came next.

"Speaking of children," I began my scenario, "my dad wants to retire. We have that cotton and citrus farm down on the border, and he's getting old and in a rut. He doesn't want to completely retire, actually. He wants me to take over the farm, and he'd show me the ropes and all it entails to run one. I know some of how to run things, from growing up on it, but not the whole business stuff and messing with the government, you know."

She stared at me more intently now.

"I'm going home, Mary Lou. My dad doesn't want to give up the farm. The land alone would help him retire if he sold it all, including the equipment. Or he could rent out the land—that's an option. If a farmer rents it and farms it, that farmer would keep three-fourth of the yield from it, while the owner of that land gets one-fourth. My mom is a high school teacher. They could make it. It would be tight, but they are used to struggle. So, money is not the issue. Keeping our farm is the issue."

"What are you going to do, then, Kaleb? Get to it."

"I wanted to talk it over with you," I answered.

She studied me more.

"So, talk," she finally said.

"I love you, Mary Lou."

"Somehow there is a 'but,' " she came back.

"No buts," I said, shaking my head. "I love you and want to marry you, but I work in a lumberyard and sing in a restaurant. So."

A smile eased onto her face.

"Kaleb, you've got a college degree. You have options. You working with your dad on a farm is wonderful, but we could still get married with or without farming and not starve. It's not a choice between working in a lumberyard or owning a farm."

She leaned to put her arms around my neck and kissed me on the lips, then nodded emphatically.

"I could only dream," she said with a sigh. "Sometimes I do dream of it, Kaleb, but I was scared to bring it up. You seemed so unsure of yourself."

"I'm sure," I replied. "I'll take over the land we own

and pay my dad and mom rent as if I was any old farmer in the area. My dad is going to need some of the equipment to custom farm in retirement. That's what he's going to do. Custom farm. He'll use our equipment to work other farmers' land when they have extra work and need extra help during peak seasons, like for planting and harvesting and cultivating. But I can use the equipment too, for our farm. I'm sure there will be conflicts at times, but he'll give our farm priority over the custom farming he intends to do."

"Wow!" She sighed. "I feel like a somebody. And don't you scold me, Kaleb. Yes, God loves me and you love me, so I'm not a nobody. But please let me feel it on my own. I'll be the wife of a *patrón* for once. Not living in a small studio apartment, not doing menial tasks, not feeling worthless and worrying about my future."

"You'll have plenty of menial tasks to help with on the farm," I answered her. "And there will be plenty of worrying to do about our future."

"Our future, Kaleb. Do you hear how glorious that sounds?"

"Yes," I answered. "And it will feel even more glorious living it. With me. In Texas."

"You rescued me right back, Kaleb. I was just doing a good deed anyone would do. You ate in our restaurant instead of being off murdering someone. Next thing you know, here I am. Ready to live on a farm. With you. The love of my life."

"I'm the love of your life?" I asked with a swoon.

"You know the answer to that. And don't act like it's a big deal, though it better be a big deal. There is so much to love about you. And here you are loving me. There was that scene in *The Sound of Music*. I know that's corny, but I loved that movie. Where Julie Andrews is ready to marry the baron or whatever he was. And she thought back on her tumultuous life and wondered what she did to deserve all this. That's me now. Like some Julie Andrews in *The Sound of Music*. Because here you are loving me."

"And feeling grateful for finding you," I replied. "It was worth being arrested."

"Oh, Kaleb, oh, oh! Oh, my God. I love you. Suddenly, I feel worthy. Yes, I'm up to this. To being your wife and raising our children and being family with your parents. The Bible talks about not having to be worthy. Just letting God love you. It's true. Here it is now, living proof. And it feels wonderful. I'll do it. I'll be up to it. We don't even have to live happily ever after. Our parents survived the Depression and the war. We'll struggle at times and discipline our naughty children sometimes. But it feels so sacred anyway."

"We'll need to tell Dale."

"He'll be happy, don't you think?"

"We'll have to be fair to him," I mused. "Give him time to find someone. Not just anyone, but let him be selective. To feel good about whoever and not just grab anyone out there. He's a hard taskmaster, and even if he gets someone good, there are going to be some problems."

"So, I have my birth certificate," she said. "You have yours, or your passport, for sure, I mean. Let's register now. Even today, or the first time we get the chance."

"You're beautiful when you're happy, Mary Lou."

"You'd better be ready to see a whole lot more of it, Mr. Kaleb, my husband."

Chapter Eighteen

I've met women who greatly moved me. Women I had a great deal of affection for, so much that I wanted to be with them and could picture happiness with them. But my independence-oriented antibodies eventually zoomed in to cure me of potential folly. Nothing, not even women, matched adventure for me. Anywhere.

Did this mean I wasn't really prepared to settle down now with Mary Lou? I'd felt domestication challenges in my psychological DNA of late—because of her. Was it pure coincidence that Mary Lou and my settling down urges coincided? Women were always wonderful. Not just alluring, but wonderful. There were exceptions, but women were always better than music for calming any savage beast inside me. And just another reason to adore them.

But.

There was a world out there to conquer. Some exotic and challenging places to tease me. And those places had women too. That seemed to answer that, until I started hitchhiking home on my last leg of going around the world. And until I needed someone to rescue my very life. Then, to see her struggles from needless self-doubt, and for me to rescue her gratefully in return. It all created a wonderful interdependency between us. Perhaps none of this interdependency would have occurred had I not been ready to settle down. To bother now to finally take seriously a life essential whose time had come for me. Even to cherish the thought of children someday. These fulfillments now invaded my life, like a prophet bringing forth enlightenment. It seemed spiritual to feel all this.

We chose to not yet tell Dale about our plans. We weren't that sure about our plans, after all. Just that we *wanted* plans and were sure we would have them eventually. We wanted to settle into them and gain rapport with them. To live day to day with them and see things in a different light than what had presented itself previously. It felt like maturity going on inside me at last. Little old me, suddenly growing up and realizing how something so important was at last an enlightenment inside me!

"Your songs are sweeter lately," Dale said to us one day during a work break. "My wife says it's because you two are in love."

"We've been in love for several weeks," we responded in unison.

"Not like now," he said.

We all looked over at Jose.

"It's true, *amigo*," Jose concurred. "You know what you want now. Both of you do."

Mary Lou and I glanced at each other quickly with a smirk. It was so obvious to everyone, and it was going over well.

"How much longer are you going to be working with us?" Dale asked. "You're both welcome to stay as long as you like. You both work well and you brighten up the place, too. I hate to see you go, but it's obvious you need better than here. Better than here should be your highest priority."

"We talk about it some," I answered. "My dad wants

me to come home and take over the farm."

Everyone looked at Mary Lou.

"Does that set with you?" Dale asked.

"It's a nice thought," she remarked. "So down to earth, excuse the pun. I'd feel so productive to even consider being a housewife on a farm."

"You'd get sucked into the operation somewhere," Dale replied. "And so would your kids. All that is good, but you have to be up to it."

"It has an appeal to me," she said.

"Us settling down is so obvious?" I asked while studying our friends and their reactions.

"Listen to this guy," Jose said with a chuckle. "Everyone falls in love. You two are domesticated now, and it's because of each other. Like you've been married for years."

Mary Lou blushed. "Should we tell them?" she asked, looking at me.

"We've done the paperwork and found a court," I said. "We're getting married next week. We don't fully know the day yet. We wanted to make sure that both of us being gone a couple of days wouldn't put a strain on the lumberyard operations."

"Somehow, you two being gone would mean everything falls apart?" Dale said with a laugh. "We might get some real work done for a change! Listen, I'm suspending both of you with pay for Wednesday and Thursday next week. So, do what you want with those two days, but I better not see you."

Everyone laughed.

"So, Dale," Mary Lou said shyly, "can you and your wife and Jose come to the wedding? A small one. Just you three as our witnesses. Then you can go back to work here. We don't need a honeymoon."

"We'll be there," he answered. "Just give us the time and place. And you most definitely are getting a honeymoon. Would you like to go to the Grand Canyon? On me. Or Monument Valley? It's not all that far away. Well maybe far enough, I guess."

"Oh, no," she said, while touching his forearm. "We don't need anything fancy. We'll be going to Texas in a month. That will be our real honeymoon. In my car, small as it is. Neither of us owns anything. We'll get to the Rio Grande at El Paso and follow it to his home on the Gulf of Mexico. We'll just do a couple of hundred miles a day, for the most part. Summer will be over by then, and it will be a nice trip even though I don't have air conditioning in my car."

"Well, I'm getting you air conditioning," Dale exclaimed. "No one is going across these deserts with their windows down."

"Dale, seriously," she appealed. "The summer is over. I have to finish the semester, and that's just before Christmas. The worst of the heat is gone. It'll be cold at night, but we'll be in a motel by then. I love natural air. I prefer it."

"Dale," I came in, "I'm a Marine. Not only that, but I grew up on a farm in south Texas, where we had to work ten hours or more in the Texas sun without an air-conditioned cab. I couldn't live with myself if I had an air conditioner. My father would never let me live it down if we had air-conditioning in our car."

Dale looked at me, showing approval.

"Marines are the greatest," he said. "I needed to learn the ropes of running the lumberyard when coming out of high school. My father didn't want me joining any military, especially with the Vietnam War raging. But I wanted to join the Marines and now I feel so left out for *not* joining. The Cong never stood a chance with guys like you in the Marines."

"Hey, *cabrón*, are you sure you're not Mexican?" Jose chided.

The week flew by. We felt thoroughly accepted by our friends in the lumberyard. Soon we would begin our trek to my home. But first, we would share getting married with our friends in Tucson, Arizona, the place that spawned our happiness.

"Dale," I chirped in a joking manner as we drove to the wedding. "Your yard help needs to be my best man. This guy named Jose, you probably know him. It's a small wedding. A justice-of-the-peace wedding. But your wife is here too. It's set up. We only need us, the JP, and two witnesses, but now we have your wife too. So, we've got a best man now and two best men won't work out, so you'll have to be the one giving away the bride. You'll just have to say 'I do' when the JP asks who's doing that. We'll have a matron of honor, with your wife. She can handle Mary Lou's ring, and Jose can handle mine. That's not a big deal. It's still a small wedding. Straightforward. We'll bother with a little formality too."

"I'm going to handle the ring, you say?" chirped Jose as we parked the car in front of the courthouse.

I nodded and handed it to him as we departed the car and walked into the office of the Justice of the Peace. Mary Lou retrieved her ring from her blouse pocket and handed it to Dale's wife.

"This isn't a ring," Jose scoffed as he inspected it after I gave it to him. "It's a washer for one of bossman's bolts."

"Not far off," I replied with a laugh. "Mary Lou and I went to a discount store that had jewelry. We barely had money for even these cheapies. But someday, when we're established and rich, we'll get diamonds or something."

"No, we won't," Mary Lou countered forcefully. "This is my wedding band for the rest of my life, and I'm giving both of our rings to our children proudly for posterity. I love my ring."

"Hear, hear," Dale's wife praised. "Yes, you are one hundred percent right, my dear. These are wonderful and cherished rings for the both of you."

"We're all wearing dress clothes for this," Mary Lou noted. "If the ceremony got any more formal now, we'd be underdressed."

"I didn't want a tuxedo," I said. "They're not only expensive but uncomfortable, too. All the more reason for a simple JP wedding. Look respectable, but not fancy. Among friends. But having a best man is nice. A special memory of Tucson. And now a matron of honor. That is better than such a simple wedding that we only have two witnesses and the JP. So, wearing Sunday clothes but not-so-fancy clothes is perfect."

There was a couple getting married just ahead of us when we arrived at the JP court. We saw the last minutes of it. The young couple didn't bother with two witnesses. Those were supplied by employees of the JP court. It was over quickly.

We presented our documents, and after everyone was introduced, we proceeded to the ceremony. As straightforward and businesslike as the JP was, my emotions began to churn. I had cried openly at both of my sisters' weddings, and was determined not to do so at my own, but when my time came I was too choked up to say the words "I do." Mary Lou looked at me with concern, as if wondering whether I was suddenly getting cold feet.

"Oh, these Marines," Jose sneered at me mockingly. "So macho. He's ready to cry, *mi amigo* here."

"Do I say I do for him?" Dale asked with a laugh.

The words came out from me after all, and we were married.

"It was sweet," Dale's wife said as we walked out to the car. "I got choked up just watching them, and then when Kaleb got emotional, I had to fight tears of my own."

"That's the most beautiful wedding I've ever been a part of," Dale said. "Except for my own. And it probably cost a nickel to have it. This is how weddings should be."

"Just two young people wanting to sacredly spend the rest of their lives together," Dale's wife added.

Dale looked at Mary Lou and me.

"We're going to the lumberyard," he said. "My dad and my daughter prepared a little feast for you. A wedding gift from us to you. You're only here a few more weeks, until Mary Lou is through with her college semester. You said you're not going anywhere until you leave, but your lease is up at the end of the semester and you'll leave right away after that. So, we want to send you off into your marriage and your journey to Texas with this celebration now at the yard. Nothing fancy, just good food. No booze, though. That's still a rule."

As we arrived at the office of the lumberyard, the staff greeted us, led by Dale's daughter, who hugged us.

"I needed to stay here and take care of the reception

rather than go to the wedding," she told Mary Lou. "That's why Dad told you he put me on some kind of mission only I could do and so couldn't spare me. Weak as that excuse may be, it was so I could take charge of the reception. It made me feel special."

Mary Lou hugged her again. "Oh," she said with an emotional sigh, "I am so honored by your caring to do that. You have been here for me the whole time. I may not have gotten this job except for you. You just know you were invited and wanted at the wedding even though this was more important and I cherish you all the more for it."

Someone blared out the song "Take My Hand for a While" by Buffie Sainte-Marie from a cassette tape. That got Mary Lou and me emotional again. As sad as the words of the song were, we had a happy occasion to share with it. Buffy would be proud, we were sure. The heartbreak in the song as we heard it being played instead turned into a celebration of love and happiness for us all. The sincerity of the love was moving. Ours felt like the best wedding anyone had ever had.

Chapter Nineteen

Mary Lou gave one last look at what had been our first home together as she drove her small, loaded car out to the street and headed for I-10. Thus began our journey to my waiting family farm in south Texas. We looked at one another with our hearts in our eyes, then focused on the road ahead—our road to destiny.

"What's going to be our song?" she asked as she pulled onto the freeway. "Do you realize we never came up with a song for us?"

"Yes, we did," I countered. "And you know that."

She looked at me curiously.

" 'Take My Hand for a While,' " I informed her.

"That's not an 'our song' type song," she returned. "It is sentimental to us, but it's about a long-lost love."

"All the better. It makes it perfect. It's about huge, enduring and endearing love. A 'better to have loved and lost than never to have loved at all' type of love. It's wonderful. Even the pain."

She looked at me and smiled.

"You're the best time I ever had," she said.

"And that's why you married me."

She nodded enthusiastically.

The highway was long and redundant, but we were on a mission. An exciting one because we were etching out our story together. By noon we passed a sign stating we had just entered the Land of Enchantment. We were now in New Mexico.

"You know," I said to Mary Lou as she drove, "New Mexico is so pretty. All these open-range natural monuments God put here. I've seen pictures of them, but I thought, yeah, well, they found something pretty somewhere. But New Mexico being called the Land of Enchantment? Well, it really and truly is."

We barely spoke the rest of that day's drive, and we reached the Texas border a few hours later. We were mesmerized by all we saw. This was the narrowest part of New Mexico, and we were beginning to regret we didn't take a longer route. We wanted more of this truly enchanting state.

"El Paso is so dry that a lot of people don't like it," I told Mary Lou as we entered that historic city at the far western extremity of Texas. "My mother hates it here. But it's on the Rio Grande. That alone makes me love it. There's an important Army base here that helped win the West and created stability. There's a university that won a national championship in basketball. And there's the Davis Mountains that are part of the Rocky Mountain chain. El Paso is isolated, but it's a fair-sized city that provides jobs and fills needs. I don't know what people want. My mother isn't into nightlife, so that's not the issue with her. It has no bright alluring lights. It does have a lot of arid terrain, and that's all some people see. The nots, not the wonders."

"Oh, my God," she said with a sigh. "Is our whole marriage going to be like this? I sure hope so. A tour guide of a husband here."

The best part of the trip, to me, was crossing the Pecos River and following it down to Interstate 90. I talked myself out of going to Big Bend National Park. It was so far out of the way for us that it seemed a waste to go that far south just to take a couple of pictures and then run off again to get back onto the interstate. Someday, just someday, maybe we would do all of that. Perhaps a second honeymoon when we could spend some time there.

I-90 was south enough to see the Pecos River begin to widen. Dark blue remnants of melted snow flowed in it, down from far away mountains, making it so much wider as it approached the Rio Grande.

"I know we're in a hurry, Kaleb, and it's so beautiful that I'm getting a lot out of it. It's such a tease to not wallow in the scenery here. Instead we just watch it roll by us."

"It gets better," I replied. "As much as I like the Pecos River, my favorite part of this far west region of Texas is the town of Alpine. It's a college town. But it's situated in an adorable mountain terrain so there's this little oasis of a town right smack dab in the middle of a semi-barren region in a mountain belt. It's so isolated. But what a place to be stuck! Maybe I'm the only one who likes it. Adores it. We'll see. Let's have supper there and continue on. This will be our last night on the road. I'll call my dad and say we're arriving late afternoon tomorrow."

Traveling in open areas of nature like far west Texas overwhelmed my senses. It wasn't just God all around, but history's ghosts abounded, too. Especially the Indians. There were no Indian reservations around as there were in nearby New Mexico. The only Indian reservation in Texas is toward the eastern part of the state. Yet I could feel the Indians as I drove. They were here. With their lances and their teepees or whatever they lived in out here a hundred or so years ago. Here we were in their vast open spaces with a universe of stars above as I took my turn driving Mary Lou's car. This was a glorious honeymoon, even if spent in a small car.

"We're approaching hill country," my tour guide lecture continued hours later. "I'd love to stop in Junction, but it's best not to. We're too far north on I-10. It's on the outside edge of hill country. I entered my college career there at the Texas A&M adjunct campus. I was just out of high school and wanted to go to Junction. It's a small town but a pretty area. It's called Junction because the Llano and Frio Rivers join there. A junction of rivers. Texas A&M had a small campus at the adjunct for civil engineers to practice surveying and whatever. A few courses were taught besides, to make sure no one wasted a semester just doing a bit of surveying and such in the semi-desert. They have real classes there, but only a few. Entering freshmen could also go there to concentrate on studies instead of being overwhelmed by college social life. We were all housed in Quonset huts, which was fine because that's what we wanted to go to A&M for. The rough life. Farm boys, blue-collar families, a place for their sons. A&M was mostly male and military back then. Quonset huts with no air-conditioning in a Texas summer out in hill country. That wasn't fun. Except we were used to not-fun environments. A&M was a hardy place back in the ol' Army days. So, entering freshmen who went to the Junction campus for summer school got their first taste of college in that environment. Junction is probably most famous, though, for when first year A&M coach Paul 'Bear' Bryant needed a getaway to train the football team with his hard-core style. He needed to get away from the hounding of the press and alumni who wanted an immediate national championship. Four busloads of football players entered the A&M adjunct in the summer of 1954 and he ran everybody off—eliminated them from the team—including the all-Southwest Conference center. Of the four full buses of football players who entered Junction, only half a busload remained to go back to College Station. I love being associated with Junction because of that."

"Is our marriage going to be like this, Kaleb?" Mary Lou asked with a chuckle. "Say that it is, sweetheart. I'm glad you know more than 'Columbus discovered the Americas in 1492.' You seem to know something about every place we've been."

"Then there's the author O. Henry," I continued, undismayed. "He was in hill country near here. Castroville. It's out of the way from the route we're taking, though."

"*The Cisco Kid*," she chirped. "I used to watch all those reruns. I remember the author O. Henry wrote that. The same guy that wrote *The Gift of the Magi*."

"You're great, Mary Lou. I'm loving it. Look at you! An active mind inside you there. O. Henry had a sense of irony that was wonderful in his stories. "Castroville is not far away. You want to go?"

"Don't, Kaleb," she howled. "Don't! I love it, but don't. My brain can't hold anymore!"

"Well, we'll be at my dad's farm in a few more hours. You won't have to put up with very much more of the sentimental me."

"It'll be work, work, work, won't it?" she asked point-blank. "But I have the feeling you'll make that interesting too. Are your parents like you? I'll feel surrounded."

"No one's like me," I replied.

That brought a smile of approval on her face for my self-analysis. Honeymoons were great.

"We're still hugging the Rio Grande River region," I explained to Mary Lou as she drove us. "It keeps going east while veering south. It lets us bypass San Antonio, which is on I-10. We'll get to a decent-sized town soon. Then it's another four hours to home from there. It's getting late. Do you want to spend one more night on the road or continue on? If we keep going I'm afraid some of the motels will be closed in these sparse areas. Less options—and out here we don't want sparser options."

"I'm pretty fatigued from the last couple of days," she replied. "Another four hours traveling tires me just thinking about it. Then we'll meet your parents and then unpack." She looked at me to let what she said sink in. "Let's stop, and we'll start fresh in the morning."

"Okay, we'll stop one more time. That means we didn't advance very far today. We're not going so direct now, because I wanted to show you more of Texas. But we can spoil ourselves because we're on our honeymoon and all. Texas is your new home. Welcome to Texas! It's so cowboy out here too. It's wonderful to show you this! This is so much the place everyone thinks about when picturing Texas. Del Rio is closest to where we are now, as far as a decent-sized town with some accommodation. Or we could go on to Brackettville. Brackettville's not very large. But…" I looked at her and smirked. "It's more interesting."

"How's that?" she asked, as if on cue.

"There's a Hollywood village there. Actually, there's an old Army fort there. And a nice cave they made a recreational site out of. But the interesting thing about Brackettville is Alamo Village."

"I thought the Alamo is in San Antonio."

"It is, but John Wayne made an Alamo Village in Brackettville patterned after San Antonio of 1836. It includes a replica of the Alamo. Like the one the Texans fought in. The real Alamo standing now in San Antonio is just a small portion of the original structure from back then. San Antonio today is over a million people and the second largest city in Texas, even bigger than Dallas. In contrast, at Alamo Village you'll get a sense of the original Alamo and the San Antonio that was the main city in Texas at the time of the Republic. Alamo Village is pretty authentic in a historical sense—thank you, John Wayne. It's a tourist site now. They have shows there about those times, 1836 and all. It makes the locals want to keep the Hollywood village alive. A tourist draw. Brackettville doesn't even have two thousand residents, so they need the tourism."

"So, 'tourists' means motels."

"Not that many, but we'll find one. Worst case scenario, we can drive all the way to Harlingen, my hometown."

She nodded enthusiastically.

"While we're in Brackettville we can walk around the village in the morning before we do our last stretch of traveling," I added. "I feel so Texan here. Because of the whole area, but mostly because of the history Alamo Village presents."

"All as part of my new home," she returned with a smile. "It'll help acclimate me."

"We'll be refreshed and energized, too, because of the history. And then we'll be home soon after that and ready to meet our future."

"Our future together," she said with a sigh.

We shared a smile.

"They have little clubs in Brackettville," I mentioned. "I'm not sure they are open this time of year, but probably so. Clubs like a restaurant but with entertainment, you know. I want to say like Moonshine where we used to sing, but these here are more family-oriented, even especially for children. There's singing like you and I did in Moonshine. Johnny Rodriguez got his start there. I thought about doing what he did in Brackettville. I sent in a tape once and got politely rejected. Sent in another the next year and got rejected again. I didn't know if I really wasn't good enough or if it was the cassette tape I used. Happy Shahan, the guy that ran the Village, told me my tape was the problem. He didn't even listen to either one of them, he told me later after I looked him up. He wanted me to sing into a reel-to-reel tape recorder. So, blame Happy Shahan for my staying undiscovered."

"Or blame you for not getting a reel-to-reel," she countered, grinning.

"If you want to look at it that way," I said with a chuckle.

We drove by Alamo Village but decided not to stop after all. Travel fatigue was setting in and we wanted to get to my home in Harlingen sooner. So we settled for glimpses of the village and then continued onward.

"So, Mary Lou, we've made it to Uvalde by mid-evening. Uvalde was the home of former Vice President John Nance Garner, who was the first VP of President Franklin Roosevelt. Uvalde was also the childhood home of actress Dale Evans, wife of the King of the Cowboys,

Roy Rogers. She wrote their theme song, called 'Happy Trails To You.' Uvalde is a small town, but big enough for motel rooms, especially since it's one of the few sizable towns in the region."

"I am ready for a motel, Kaleb," she said with relief. "It's been a long day."

As we entered the city limits of Uvalde, I slowed down and looked at Mary Lou.

"I'm checking into this motel. It seems well taken care of and looks cheap enough."

She nodded as if to give me benefit of the doubt. After checking in, we brought in our suitcases to the small motel room with its single window air-conditioning unit.

"The next town is Sabinal," I explained later as we relaxed in our room. "Sabinal is where country singer Johnny Rodriguez was from. I thought about spending the night there, just to do so because of him. But Sabinal is small and it's late now, so I didn't want to gamble on whether we'd find anything. This is maybe my favorite part of Texas, not counting where I grew up, or Texas A&M, my alma mater. This is all hill country. We have mountains in the far west of Texas, as you've seen. But Texas is mostly flat. Between Austin and San Antonio, though, and just west of them, are beautiful rolling hills like we're viewing. So, 'Hill Country.' There's a lot of German descendants because of it. German immigrants started coming here in the mid-nineteenth century because of political unrest in Germany. They liked the hill country because it was green and the rolling hills reminded them of home in Germany."

"You are so sentimental," Mary Lou teased. "People just find a place. You have all these memories, no matter what, to add to whatever we do. And here we are traveling with John Nance Garner, Dale Evans, and Johnny Rodriguez, you might say."

"I came home from the Marine Corps," I reminisced aloud for Mary Lou's benefit. "Got processed out at Camp Pendleton. So, musing about my life now that I was out of the Marines, I tried to absorb home again—my upbringing and how things were now. I was lying in bed my first night back and listening to the radio a bit, to relax before dozing off, and pretty soon some guy began singing in Spanish. I looked again at the station number I'd tuned to. There was supposed to be a country station at this spot. It was a pretty song, but it made me wonder what was going on. Then, very early in the song, right after the intro, this guy started singing in English. It was an old country song, remade into a bilingual one for a country audience. I had been gone only a year, so it had me wondering what else was going on around here. Turns out the singer was a Hispanic country singer. The guy we know well as Johnny Rodriguez. Being from south Texas, I was charmed, but it also made me wonder if country music was losing its way."

"Yes, Johnny Rodriguez," Mary Lou sighed at the memory. "He was unique and gave country a new outlet. A bigger one. Next thing you know, there's the Texas Tornados and Freddy Fender."

"You're wonderful," I praised. "We'll be happy here."

"Exactly the thing we should be," she replied. "To be together with your family and all of us happy."

"Yeah," I said with a smile of approval. "Perfect."

"Are your parents going to like me?" she fretted openly. "I'm so nervous, Kaleb."

"They'll love you. They're old-fashioned and believe in family. You're family and down to earth, and a working girl."

"Yeah, but you said your mother has a master's degree. I'm a hick."

"She's a hick. An educated one. She grew up a sharecropper in west Texas, then worked as a waitress for her first job just before she got married. She was homecoming queen in high school, and valedictorian, too. Everyone else was a hick there in that part of the world, but she got to feel special a little."

"But Kaleb..." Mary Lou sighed. "You told me before how she made Who's Who in America academically while she was working on her master's. She made something of herself. She had so much self-confidence in herself even if still a farm girl."

"Yeah," I replied. "It even gave me confidence, knowing all this stuff about her. For every self-doubt inside me, I could remember my mother with the master's degree who made academic Who's Who in America."

"I was ready to flunk out of junior college until you came along, Kaleb. She'll try to love her daughter-in-law, but what's she really going to think of me?"

"She'll love you, and that's a start. I did happen along in your life, though, and you passed your semester in junior college after all. You're not finished with success, either. You'll take it more seriously now and get your bearings and you'll see who you really are. Success takes on a life of its own."

She looked at me in a serious but loving way.

"It's already started," she said. "Just being with you makes me feel special."

"And now comes the rest of the story," I answered.

Chapter Twenty

The lower Rio Grande Valley of south Texas is on the border with Mexico. The Rio Grande River flows into the Gulf of Mexico there at Brownsville, which is the southernmost city in the continental United States. Just across from it lies Mexico. My dad had a farm in this area and Mary Lou and I reached it late in the afternoon after leaving Uvalde. It felt good to be going to our family farm now, this time as an equal with my father rather than the boy helping out and taking orders while knowing he had better work hard or have hell to pay. I figured out quickly, while growing up, that working hard was appealing, in fact. Not that work was appealing of itself. I used to count the days until school started in September, knowing I would finally have a life again besides seven days a week of fourteen-hour days at hard labor on the farm. I was proud of the work I did, though, and even got to where I was glad to be raised that way. I felt like a real Texan because of it. City slickers seemed like sissies to me. They had it so easy!

Since we had a farm, we got by. It seemed we never had enough money and my dad, like all the other farmers around, had to worry if banks were going to lend to him every year so he could buy seed for crops, and fertilizer to nurture the young plants, as well as enough credit or money to maintain old equipment or perhaps buy brand-new equipment. And we had to have money to pay the hands that labored in the fields for us.

Years later, I watched Walter Cronkite give the evening news on television. Cronkite was a Texan who had a good reputation as a news journalist. So I watched him over the other newscasters on other channels. One day in 1971 I heard him talk about the poorest area in the United States. I always assumed it was somewhere in Mississippi or perhaps West Virginia. As it turned out, it was the lower Rio Grande Valley of south Texas. The very place where I grew up. For sure it was poor, and so many of the farm laborers we hired in that area were much of the reason. My area was also the one area in the whole state of Texas that had no oil. That was like piling it on, as far as misery was concerned. Across the natural border of the Rio Grande River, Mexico was even poorer. Noticeably so. This made us look almost rich.

I felt like a survivor from all this in my upbringing. And being a survivor was good. Maybe that's why I wanted to go to Vietnam as a Marine. Not just from patriotism, but to stay a survivor type even in the worst environments and maintain the confidence of one. I was proud of my upbringing, and Walter Cronkite made me even prouder as he talked about the hard conditions of Cameron, Willacy, Hidalgo and Starr Counties, which made up most of the lower Rio Grande Valley. Farm after farm of hardy survivors. Survivors who considered hard work as sacred as the Bible.

What would Mary Lou think of this farm she was to inherit with me? She'd had a hard survivor's life too. But now she was part of this link with my family farm. Her background would help her appreciate her new home.

And how would my parents feel about her? That was the concern we were ready to face. Right away. They would want to love her and try to love her. But would they see her as a waitress with little education? They might do that even though my mother was a waitress once, in her survival days. My parents had survived worse things than I ever had to put up with, and it was engrained in them to demand more of their children to make sure our situation improved. Would they think I married a loser?

But coming home defaulted into warm secure feelings for me, with a lot of memories to back that up. Still, there was a generation gap in the mix too. I was old-fashioned and loved traditional Texas, though aware of faults in our system that the generation gap brought out. Sometimes my parents seemed rigid in their ways. They had been the ones who nurtured me, but at times I felt suffocated by outlooks from them that seemed more memorized as law than something fully valued and understood.

I was an adult now. One they needed in their lives. I expected respect for that. And I had a college degree from a major university, a factor that at least gave some credence to my viewpoints. We would be trying hard with one another for idealistic as well as practical reasons. But would there be family cohesion among us?

"We just crossed Combes Mountain," I said with a chuckle after turning onto the state highway that would lead us to our farm.

"What mountain?" she asked.

I didn't answer immediately, to make her curiosity venture a guess as to what I was referring to. She stared at me as she waited for my reply, then turned to look back at where we just had been.

"That little hump that supported the railroad track?"

she asked while shaking her head. "That's what you're talking about? That's your mountain?"

"And the little village we passed through is called Combes," I related.

"Combes Mountain, eh?" She giggled. "Okay. Ha. I'll be sure to go skiing there this coming winter."

"It's semi-tropical here," I explained. "It never snows. Or if it does, it melts before it hits the ground. So the good news is we have very mild winters. The bad news is we have very long summers."

"I'm sure I'll complain sometimes, but I do like the sun, so that trumps not getting to ski."

"I like the sun too," I concurred. "There are times I'm so sick of the cold, I swear I'll never complain of summer heat again. Then I complain anyway after a few ninety-degree or hundred-degree days. But there are almost no cold days after February here, and our true fall weather doesn't begin until just before Thanksgiving. It's already hot by May and damn hot by June, and it stays that way until October. It stays hot, though not all that hot, in October and November and is even a bit hot in December. Retired people from up north flock here in the fall and stay through most of the spring. Seems like every winter it gets down into the forties a few days, and every few years down into the thirties. It even gets below freezing every so often. I used to feel sorry for the Yankees here trying to stay warm and then this happens to them."

"Until you lived up north with the cold there," she said as if to finish my sentence.

"Yeah. Yeah. My God, I missed home in all that Yankee cold."

"So, it's almost Christmas," she mused. "Sounds

like we're just in time for perfect weather here in the semi-tropics."

I nodded and gave a wink. Mary Lou turned in her seat toward me, but still looked through the windshield straight ahead, inspecting her new environment.

"We're almost there," I informed her. "We just passed a little village that doesn't have much more than a convenience store and a handful of houses. The kids here all went to the same elementary school I did. It's a few miles down the road that was perpendicular to us there. We were all hicks, but didn't know it because of all the stories we heard about hillbillies in surrounding states. Somehow, we were normal and they were hicks. Turns out we were just as bad."

"I saw orchards along the way. You told me about oranges and those Ruby Red variety grapefruit from here. So you're just like California."

I looked at her and smirked, then shook my head emphatically.

"I'm glad we both have citrus," I answered, almost sneering, "but no, we aren't anything like California. You'll catch on real quick."

My focused attention stared into the distance.

"This is it," I said. "We're here. You'll notice all the houses are at least a quarter mile apart. Not quite like Daniel Boone, but when we say neighbors, we don't mean like next door. There's fields and pasture land around each house."

"You don't feel isolated?"

"Harlingen is the big city in these parts. Forty thousand people. Combes has six hundred people, and that village we just now passed has about fifty people. The next town on this highway has eighteen hundred. It's pretty settled here because there're so many farmers. You don't have to have big sprawling acreage here because the land is so good and there's abundant water. So, even though it's all agriculturally oriented, the farms don't make up large estates. We have these little settlements in between a few moderately sized towns. I don't feel isolated at all. And we have cars. We work hard and don't go to town all that much, but it's there nearby and there's a need to go often enough. You feel like part of it all. Alone somewhat, but not isolated."

She nodded her head and turned back into her seat, facing straight ahead again as I turned into our driveway.

"A brick house," she commented. "I'm almost disappointed. It seems like an estate after all."

"We do okay. Like I say, it's poor here, but we were good farmers. Both my parents grew up sharecroppers in the Depression and they have a drive in them to not ever look back. They made the farm work. It's very fertile and irrigated land. Farming is so productive here in this region because of that. Mother nature helps out, too. Cotton, corn, maize, orchards, vegetables, cattle… You can even grow vegetables in the winter. An agricultural area all the west Texans talked about during the war— down south by Mexico, the lower Rio Grande Valley area, flat land, flood irrigation with good rich soil, paradise—so my dad came home a war hero and used the G.I. Bill to buy fifty acres to give him a start. He had a small wooden house on those fifty acres, to raise a family."

"The American dream," she quipped.

"They invented the American dream."

"But Kaleb," she mused aloud, "even with good land and lots of water, you can't raise a family or even survive on your own with only fifty acres."

"But it means you have something to show you're working hard, and it's collateral for loans. And you need loans. There is so much farmland here and so little industrialization that land is cheap and you can rent from those who own a few acres, but work in town. They love owning land, and it supplements their income. Rent for that land comes to one-fourth of the harvest. They rent their land out to farmers like my dad. No expense for them except property tax, and not much of that because of agricultural deferments."

"A can't-miss," she quipped.

"Nothing about a farm is a can't-miss," I answered. "I remember once when I worked with my dad the whole summer, hoeing cotton—we call it chopping cotton—spraying for pests, picking cotton, the first picking by hand, then the second or, if needed, a third, these done by machine. You defoliate to make the cotton mature faster at the end. And we have our grain and corn fields—planting, chiseling, cultivating, harvesting. Also our Ruby Red orchards—the only place on earth when I was growing up that produced Ruby Red grapefruit. It not only has red meat inside, different from the other varieties, but it's a bit sweeter than the other varieties. I remember times when we did all this farm work, twelve-hour days or more at times, seven days a week at peak season...and then a hurricane wiped out most of our crops."

"You're scaring me, Kaleb."

"Don't be scared. But be ready."

At the end of our long driveway was our house. I parked to the side of our garage, under a mesquite tree.

"I'm so nervous, Kaleb," Mary Lou said, fretting.

"Especially with all your stories. My dad ran off when I was little. My mom struggled to raise us the whole time. We're white trash. Uneducated white trash. I've got some college, but I struggle to get by even though I went to a local community college. Your mom was a Who's Who. Your dad was a war hero who owns a brick house. They're going to think you got me pregnant or something and had to marry me."

I looked at her and smiled reassuringly.

"They've made something of themselves," I said to her. "They can judge harshly at times, but mostly, they know who they are and where they came from and what it took to have anything to show for it. They'll love you. Especially when they get to know you."

I looked reassuringly at Mary Lou again and nodded for us to get out of the car.

"Will they expect you to open the door for me?" she asked showing her nervousness more.

"We are courteous to women here," I replied. "But we don't baby anyone. Opening a door or pulling out a chair for a lady is often expected, but they expect women to fend for themselves usually. Anyway, we have our suitcases. Hands full, ya know. I'll knock to prepare them we're here. They probably heard me drive up. They know we're arriving about now, from when I called them yesterday. They'll greet us and show us the room where we'll be staying. We'll get to know one another."

"Oh, Kaleb, I'm such a coward. That's what I'm afraid of. They'll get to know me way too much for comfort."

"You're insulting my judgment of character," I told her.

Chapter Twenty-One

Mary Lou's nervousness was obvious as my father opened the door to the front of the house.

"This is Mary Lou, my new wife," I said, smiling broadly, proud of her. "Your new daughter-in-law."

Both my father and my mother picked up on her nervousness and my intervention to make her feel at home.

"Mother," Mary Lou said before reaching out to hug her.

My mother graciously pulled back after the hug to look at her with assurance.

"We're so proud to have you, Mary Lou," my mother said, seemingly very nervous herself now.

They hugged again.

"It's good to meet you, Mary Lou," my father greeted. "It's about time somebody settled Kaleb down. He's thirty years old and still traipsing around wearing a backpack like some hippie. So, you're the one that brought him back to earth."

"He's done as much for me," she replied.

"A match made in heaven," my mother added.

It was a nice touch that eased Mary Lou's anxiety. My parents came through, just as I knew they would.

"Do you need help unloading your car?" my father asked us.

"This is everything," Mary Lou and I answered in

unison.

Both of my parents shared expressions between humor and the pathetic.

"Mary Lou," my mother said with a grin, "we were hoping you would domesticate him more than this. One suitcase each for you two?"

"My car is so small, Mother," she said showing awkwardness. "What I didn't give away is in storage until we get settled here. Someday we'll go back and get everything we left behind."

"I suppose that makes sense, except that Tucson is so far away," my father said in a comforting manner.

"Let's show them their room," my mother said to distract from the awkwardness. "It's the same room Kaleb used to have when he lived here."

"But it's just temporary," my father explained. "Not that we feel cramped, but I got y'all a two-bedroom mobile home. It will be delivered soon. Call it a Christmas present. Or a wedding gift. Never mind. It will still have to be hooked up to plumbing and electricity, so you'll still need this room for a week or two, probably. Maybe more. There's no rush to move into the mobile home anyway. We could even use the new home for guests and you just stay with us in the house. But, when you ever do get the remainder of your things, Mary Lou, you'll have plenty of room for them."

"A mobile home?" Mary Lou swooned. "Our first-ever home! Not counting my apartment back in Tucson."

"Let me show Kaleb around," my father said. "He knows our place and all, but now that he's going to be running things along with me, I want to show him more details than before. He's lived everywhere but here for most of his adult life, and I'm going to be handing more and more responsibility to him. I've got a few more productive years ahead of me, so there's no rush, but it would be good to reorient him."

"That can wait," my mother said to him. "They had a long trip. If you've already brought in your belongings, just enjoy the rest of the day. Mary Lou can help me prepare supper soon. Just to get her acquainted with the place and feel at home. You'll have your own place soon enough, like we said."

All this attention was the medicine we needed to feel our new life together was official. All the warm feelings I had growing up were renewed in these few beginning moments of our first day as a family together. Country people knew how to make you feel right at home. Which was exactly what my parents had in mind.

"So, hey," I broke in, "we're on Christmas break now. Y'all sort of are, now, too, right? Are you planting winter vegetables?"

"Cabbage," my dad answered. "Only twenty acres. I can handle that myself. The hands are back in Mexico. Things are easy for now. Especially with you here. I can do it without you, and have in the past. But you're a welcome sight even for this. It puts less pressure on me, though it's only twenty acres. But besides that twenty acres of cabbage, I'm using the breaking plow this time of year to loosen up the soil, before the spring planting."

"That's why I'm bringing all this up now. Mary Lou was a part-time student at a junior college back in Tucson. She had to support herself as a waitress and help out her ailing mother, too. She has a sister who helps take care of their mother, but Mary Lou helped out some with money, tight as it was with her. So, right now, Mary Lou has no means of direct support. She's here on the farm now, but I'm trying to get my bearings on all this. We haven't talked much because of being just married and here we are now in Texas, but it's the off season here, and unless you need her on the farm or around the house or something, she wants to find a job. Even to pay for storing our few belongings in Tucson. We love that we have free rent now, that'll help us. But we need some income, too. She could work as a waitress, probably, since that's what she's been doing. We don't want to depend on y'all to pay our bills, so she needs a way to earn money while I work fulltime here on the farm. Unless you have a better idea. And then too, she needs to get back into school as soon as possible."

"Well, there's Pan American and there's Texas Southmost," my mother said, looking at Mary Lou.

"Yes, I've mentioned those to her," I said. "We'll need to talk to them right away."

"I don't know what all Kaleb told you," my mother said, looking to Mary Lou, "but Southmost is a junior college and it's about thirty miles away. You have a car. Pan Am is about the same distance, a little closer, and it's a four-year university. It's up to you. We can make calls and you can talk to them and then see what you decide. Are you going to be a full-time student?"

"I probably should take just three courses, to begin with," Mary Lou replied. "Until I'm more settled."

"What is it you want to study?" my mother asked her.

"No major yet, Mother. Like Kaleb was saying, I was just a part-time student in Tucson at a local junior college, because of having to work to pay for school and also to help my family."

"Well, all that is admirable, Mary Lou," my mother

said straightforwardly, nodding her head in approval. "You have a semester or two to get a feel and decide. You will have to travel thirty minutes up and thirty minutes back, so wrap your class schedule around that and working here some on the farm or as a waitress."

"All this is becoming more real to you now, isn't it, Mary Lou?" I asked. "It will all fall into place soon."

But most of the decisions were already made for us. We needed the smoothest road, and that meant part-time at the local junior college a half hour away while she worked towards making a home with us. Her poor grades needed attention. Finding herself was the highest priority. We both faced growing pains, but of a different ilk.

All this we faced together, which made it seem special. Our time to settle down and grow into our new environment came full throttle into each other's lives. Life laid out our plans for us, as if made in heaven. It was a thought that brought us determination.

And confidence.

Chapter Twenty-Two

"Have you decided which school you'll go to?" my mother asked Mary Lou at supper.

"The one in Brownsville," Mary Lou answered. "The junior college."

"That would be Texas Southmost then," my mother mused. "That seems the best choice. Until you get your bearings with living here, at least."

"Plus, it will be the easier of the two schools," Mary Lou added. "I struggled with the community college back in Tucson. Kaleb helped get me through, in fact. That bonded us even more. He helped me study harder and better, but gave me so much appreciation for education's importance. I've heard that all my life, but it seemed more like a sermon than an enlightenment. Just the appreciation for education that Kaleb gave me increased my focus and attitude. Then when he was there with me at night, helping me with my courses, I saw how it could be done. You don't have to be intelligent so much as seeing the need of the truth about knowledge, that it's the key to life, to everything. It's the focus. The joy, even. It inspires a lot more than the drudgery of hearing how important it is. Suddenly you are living that importance for the desire of knowledge and perspective."

My mother stared at Mary Lou as if absorbing what she said. She then looked at me with a smile, as if proud of me.

"She's got a long way to go," I said. "All this is just dawning on her—working for a goal. How it's like being made to eat your spinach when you're a kid. You eat it because you have to, even if you give a certain grudging acceptance for the need of it. It's not a rule to her anymore, to study, to work towards a goal. She's forming an awareness about it inside herself now, about the power of knowledge and skills, and of unknown horizons to journey toward."

"I have about a year," Mary Lou explained, "to finish junior college. Then I'll be ready for Pan American, the four-year university here. I must get my grades up more, which means I need to learn better study habits."

"Pan American is a full university and may want to evaluate you more, so they may not have the time to do that before school begins again anyway. You still don't have a major, which is probably best until you learn more about what you want and what's out there available for a girl with a degree. Southmost is used to the transient student. They'll check your transcript and see that you're eligible and take you the same day."

"That's the plot, Mother," I said. "You'll be there for her too. Not just me. She'll get inspired in stereo."

Both my mother and Mary Lou smiled at the thought. We were entering a new phase in our lives.

"Have you rearranged your room yet?" my mother asked us after we came back to the living room from settling into our new living quarters.

She looked at us for explanation, but we stared blankly, so she quizzed us further.

"Those same old pictures and pennants Kaleb used to hang up. It's been waiting on you all these years. Same old double bed for you two. As if we knew you'd bring home your bride someday."

"We haven't done anything but unpack our suitcases," I replied. "Our bedroom seemed like a museum to me, looking at everything in it."

I stared at Mary Lou, feeling inadequate from our lack of effort so far, then took her by the arm and led her back to our room for another try at settling in.

"The room ahead is where my sisters slept, their room," I told her as we walked beyond the dining room into the bedroom area of the house.

"So," she asked, "the room we just passed is your parents' room?"

I nodded yes as we walked farther towards our room.

"All the bedrooms are adjacent," I said. "My parents, mine, and my two sisters."

"So you were the only boy," Mary Lou surmised.

"Even the girls had to help on the farm sometimes," I explained. "Another brother would have been nice. Guys do so many things, including drive the equipment."

"Boy, they mean it when they say 'family farm.' "

"My old desk," I pointed out as we entered my childhood bedroom again. "My chest of drawers. Texas A&M and Marine Corps pennants. Both pennants I bought as I became an Aggie and then a Marine. A picture of our house from the air and outlying acreage of our farm. All this here is just like the day I left for college. All these years later. As if we're in a museum."

"It's wonderful, Kaleb," Mary Lou said. "So let's not rearrange any of it. It'll be okay. Mother will understand. She might even prefer it. Let me catch up with you on this room as you explain to me its history while it's been yours. It's like filling in years of my life for the family I never had. It's so hard to explain to you what all this does for me. It's like missing years of my life now are here to absorb, even though they aren't my personal years. They're mine now anyway. My inheritance from you as your wife. You know, like…at last, here they are for me. Through you."

"Thank you for saying that, Mary Lou," I said while turning toward her for a kiss. "When I left for A&M, and then the Marines, it felt good having this home background to keep me emotionally secure while entering different phases of my life. But now they are personal again to me. Waiting on me and greeting me happily. Coming back at me like some boomerang and needing them again. Except now they are here for you, as part of me, as part of us. They seem even more precious to me now."

"It's like all is forgiven inside me, Kaleb," she said endearingly. "All the insecurity I suffered through the years, the bitterness at times. The self-doubts. Here I am. All is forgiven in my past now. No need to feel unworthy anymore. As if it's a gift from God. Somehow, I must have done something good. To have you here beside me. My husband. Professing love. Incorporating me into your beautiful family. Now *my* family. I've said all this before, but I'm so grateful! And not just to you. To all the higher powers in the universe somehow."

"I'm glad you feel forgiven and worthy, Mary Lou. Forgiveness is so biblical. And it does feel of God."

"You've been so good to me, Kaleb, and it's because of more than that I saved your life. You've gotten that through to me. You found something in me that you genuinely cherish. I want you to be so proud of me. It gives me the confidence I've needed. It feels brand-new inside me. Because of you."

"I'm glad you see how proud I am of you, Mary Lou. It would take away if it was just me trying to convince you. You've picked so much up on your own about it."

"It started off," she related, "that your confidence in me made me appreciate myself. Yet I was doing it for you. To make you proud of me. But you got it through to me that you really are proud of me. As *me*, I mean. It got through to me that there is something to be proud of about me. It's there in me to see in myself now. Not just in you about me. Like I can do this."

Chapter Twenty-Three

I liked the way Mary Lou tried so hard with my mother. How she wanted to lessen her load with the house chores and how, after her first shopping trip with mother, she went out alone to shop for farm and family needs to save my mother the trouble. She was into farm life and wanted more of it. This included being out in the fields with me or in the shed and workshop when I had mechanical repairs or basic maintenance to do. She was not only smaller than me, but her inexperience could get her hurt by making novice mistakes. So there was a need to appreciate her enthusiasm while protecting her from that enthusiasm.

"Are you ever going to let me drive the tractor?" she asked as we came home after a day's work in a nearby field.

I was driving my dad's pickup but glanced her way and laid a hand on her shoulder. "Mary Lou," I said affectionately, "I know you're aware it can be dangerous even though it looks easy—and it usually *is* easy, but so many things can happen that could be really difficult. We have to be careful."

"I know, Kaleb, but it's exciting to me. To be out of the kitchen and in a bigger world. To work with Mother Nature. Sort of. On our terms anyway. To feel productive. I go to the supermarket now and look at all the produce. There's so much pride inside me knowing how I helped put these products out there. I'm contributing to America. This makes me feel special because I'm so much a part of America now. Working America. Productive America."

"I'm grateful there was all this work to be done now when we got here," I said as she cuddled next to me. "We came just before Christmas and we're already into January, with school starting for you in a week. In the meantime, we've had plenty of work to get you acclimated here and it will make your schooling more focused and purposeful. You're not just going to classes because you're supposed to, as if it's some duty to perform. Now it's all a part of the perspective in our lives. You'll figure out what to major in shortly, I'm sure of it."

There was no one near us going to Texas Southmost College. No companion to share the experience with Mary Lou. This meant she would be driving three times per week alone to Brownsville. The miles would accumulate and the gas would be paid totally by us alone. This would definitely strain our small budget.

"I'm taking Texas History," she told us over supper after her first day of class. "I never was much into history. All the names to remember and so many dates to memorize. But my husband is from Texas. My new family is from Texas. Texas is the Lone Star State. The one state that was a republic on its own before it signed a treaty as an equal with the United States to become part of it, and with the provision that it could choose to withdraw. The one state in the Union with that option."

"Boy, you have taken in your new environment!" My mother beamed.

"I remember things Kaleb told me before," she

reminisced. "You don't have to memorize what you enjoy. Some things you do have to memorize, I'm aware. But education is an aid to your life and thus part of growing. Not just force feeding yourself with stiff, boring facts."

"You've come a long way," I said, praising her.

"There's so much to love about education now," she explained. "The truth shall set you free. Yes! It does that for me now. It's not just a trite saying. I'm taking a course in real estate, too. Here I am on a farm, not just producing and laboring, but including property management in my new life, and allocation of resources. So economics is part of the management of it all. Business. Managing. Scientific production—real estate entails all of this. I have my bearings more about it now with things to relate with it."

"You'll have things to teach your kids," my father said. "Things you know about first-hand. Or will soon enough. And when you hear some politician talk malarky, you'll know what to say to him when he thinks you owe him your vote. He works for you. That makes more sense."

" 'He works for you' could mean how he induces the welfare state to support you," I added. "Take more money from the private sector to redistribute to the needy. The needy that need him to give it to them. To depend on him more than depending on a vibrant economy for survival. Even if some of welfare applies, you need perspective about it. The landed overlords may have been evil in feudal Europe or ancient China, but we aren't overlords. We're struggling middle-class masses with business acumen from a very complex system. The peasants don't own the land in Communist countries.

They work for the new overlords called the government and the politburo."

"I feel like an adult now," Mary Lou exuded. "Not just from being over twenty-one, but because it makes better sense now, how things work."

"You make me want to marry you all over again, Mary Lou."

****

Even in south Texas it gets cold at times in the winter months. Working at night on a tractor while dragging a breaking plow to loosen up the upper crust of our fields can be challenging when a norther blows in. The fact that we have to plow so deep means that the plow can't be very wide. Even our big tractors struggle with this kind of plowing. Long tedious strips in our fields that aren't even a yard wide must be plowed from early morning until well after dark, which means we need the tractor's headlights to light the field in front of the tractor pulling the plow. But the stars at night are so big and bright, it's like plowing to a heavenly lullaby. Mary Lou needed to study, but she demanded to ride with me at least an hour each night to take this in, sitting on the side fender as I had at times as a child.

"I want to be a farmer," she told me emphatically after a few nights of this.

She not only wanted to be a farmer's wife making meals for us, or washing grimy clothes, but she wanted to be a part of everything entailed on a farm. I began to let her drive the tractor at times while I sat on the side fender. My confidence in her was accompanied by knowing the tractor wasn't hard to handle. I had done all these things on the farm as early as junior high. Still, she was inexperienced, and you never knew when a large obstacle might be uncovered deep inside the soil, one that might sway the tractor when it came directly upon it. I knew I could grab the steering wheel in an emergency, if something unexpected like this happened. But it never did during the few times she was driving.

Every day you could see Mary Lou's confidence building, as well as her satisfaction in being part of a farming family.

"When are y'all going to give us grandchildren?" my mother asked us one night while we watched a movie. "Neither one of you bring it up. Kaleb, don't you want a son?"

"I just got married, Mother. It sounds like you want a grandchild. Mary Lou is finding her way. She was unskilled. She's finding out what she can do. That's more exciting at this stage than even a baby. She's still in her twenties. She's got plenty of time with her biological clock. Let her be happy on the farm a while. Having a baby is going to make her happy whenever we have it. But first things first."

My father looked at my mother and nodded approval of what I'd just said. My mother looked the other way.

"My grades came in," Mary Lou said one afternoon in late spring as she walked into the house after school. She was wearing a broad smile. Good news, obviously. "Straight A's," she bragged, looking first at me and then at my parents.

"We are so proud of you!" my mother said, hugging her affectionately.

"I even made the highest A in two of my classes. That real estate class was one of them. Maybe that's what I want to do instead of teach. Not sure I was wanting to be a teacher anyway. It sounds all right, but I've been thinking about my direction lately, and that real estate class really hits home for me. I'm going to start reading up on this, and talking to people. You keep hearing of all these rich real estate moguls. I'm not under the illusion I'll be rich someday, but I never thought I'd be a straight-A student, either. Even at a small junior college. Hopefully the sky's the limit. Suddenly, having a family, working on a farm, going to college, all of this has taken on a life of its own. Each one is a new chapter in my life, one at a time. Maybe real estate will be that for me too. Not to be rich, and I do want a family someday. But real estate appeals now."

Mary Lou was for real. I didn't have to be proud of her anymore. She was beyond needing support. She was my full partner.

Chapter Twenty-Four

I was lonely for Mary Lou often during our first summer together on our farm near Harlingen. She was gone every business day for summer school at Texas Southmost as a full-time student. We agreed she would be full-time in the fall too. She would then switch in the spring semester to our nearby four-year university, Pan American.

My mother had the dinner meal ready for me when I came home from the fields every noon. I knew Mary Lou would be home by suppertime when I came in for a quick bite before going back to the fields for all the harvesting we did during these summer months. Harvest time meant working seven days a week, with long hours per day, over a hundred hours each week. Mary Lou couldn't come to the fields with me anymore, like she had in our early days together. She had to study and prepare for classes and tests. We lived two separate lives now, except at night. They were short nights together since I had to work until late in the evening and then get up early in the morning. I hated looking up at the stars at night while I worked alone on the tractor. Alone without Mary Lou. I wanted her with me. But she was working for a goal, to be a real estate agent. I could not deny her that.

"When are you two going to have children?" my mother demanded yet again from us as we sat for supper one night. "Your dad and I are getting up in years. It's so great to have y'all here. We knew it would be. And we appreciate more and more that you're taking over the farm, Kaleb. Your dad needs more rest these days. It's more like he's helping you rather than you helping him on the farm now. All that is fine. But if y'all had kids, your dad and I could take care of them during the day while both of you are gone. We could help you take care of them at night, too, when you're here. When are y'all going to give us grandchildren? It needs to be while we're still able to be up and around and able to enjoy them!"

"We've been through this, Mother," I said in a huff. "We intend to have kids. But I am taking over the farm now. Just like you wanted. And Mary Lou is working toward her degree. Even with your help she would be bogged down with school and study. Any young kids right now would be a distraction."

"Then she'll be getting a job in real estate or whatever," my mother said with a whine, "and won't want kids while she's learning her job."

"We all need each other, then, don't we, Mother?" I said with a bite. "Mary Lou and I were going to move into that trailer house you got us. But we needed more room for our extra hands at certain seasons, so now these hands live in that trailer. That little cottage up the road we had for some of our hands through the years is empty because of that, and we renovated it. We didn't want to feel like we were living off you, so we were going to move in there once, if you remember, but we all need each other, so we're still here, even now. Yes, here we all are, still in this house where I grew up with you. All helping each other in our daily lives."

"You need us, Kaleb," my father said. "And not because you're newlyweds finding your way. We all are needing each other. You're doing us the favor, which is why I asked you to take over the farm to begin with. So, like your mother said, when are you going to give us grandkids—kids that can help on the farm someday like you did growing up. A Texas farm family, like the old Texas that we all grew up in. Here we are, almost like pioneers except we have big farm machinery and cars and a nice brick house."

"You make me feel bad, Pops," Mary Lou said, looking at him apologetically. "But school means so much to me… I grew up white trash, Pops. I know you know all that already, but while we're talking about all of this, I need you to understand. It means so much to me to be an honor student at a full university, making something of myself. My father, whom I barely remember, had some college, but I'll be the first one on either side of my family with a college degree. I'm studying hard and taking full semester coursework and going to summer school too. I'll be finished in a couple of years."

"Then you'll want a good job as your reward," my mother interjected again. "Instead of raising kids and helping out in the house, you'll want a job."

Mary Lou chewed on her lower lip while she thought.

"You're right in principle, Mother. But this is America and this is modern times. If something happens to Kaleb someday, I will have a skill in the real estate market and somehow survive without him. Women are needed in the workforce these days, not just at home. We're lucky here on the farm. We all get along, and we even love each other and are there for each other. You can help raise the kids, like you said. And y'all are letting me send money to my ailing mother back in Tucson. Thank you so much."

"It's your money too, dear," my mother said supportively. "You have private needs too. We're aware of it. We were paying for your storage back in Tucson until recently. Until we finally got a mover to bring it here. We had to wait for Kaleb to have a week he could spare to take care of it. But all that is done and over. Now we need grandchildren."

My mother then looked in celebration at my dad and me. "She keeps using the word 'y'all' more and more," she said approvingly, looking back at Mary Lou again, smiling. "Sweetheart," she said with a gleam in her eye, "yes, you get your degree. Help support your mother and sister. With love from their extended family in Texas. You're so one of us, Mary Lou, and we're so proud of you too. You are an honor student. You make us all so proud, especially Kaleb here, but all of us. You get that degree. You be the first one in your family with a college degree. You do everything you ever dreamed of doing, Pumpkin. We're so proud of you, and we need your happiness to complete our own."

Mary Lou and I got emotional after my mother finished that little speech. Family was the most wonderful thing God ever invented.

In my youth, growing up, I had issues with the farm. The work was hard and demanding. That made me very proud, but mostly I hated all the demands of the hard grueling days. Endless hours in the fields, doing menial, boring, repetitive work. I counted the days each summer for when school would start. I didn't like school. No one did. But it sure beat the Texas heat in a cotton field.

Yet I was grateful for the work required on the farm in those days to help our family's cause. I survived all of this in our demanding circumstances. *If it doesn't defeat you, it makes you stronger.* I felt like living proof of that trite saying. I didn't think of myself as especially sturdy. Not with my father's generation of war heroes and survivors around to look up to. I constantly heard stories about the Depression and what it took to survive and felt eternally inadequate, intimidated by my parents' generation. Anytime I wanted to whine about the heat or boll weevils or long physical hardships in the fields, their stories from back in the Depression were countlessly harped to me throughout my childhood. Any sympathy they displayed my way for struggles I had was followed with dismay or disgust for any lack of coping I displayed. I, in turn, judged my friends who didn't have to put up with living and working on a farm—wimps, all of them, for sure.

Mary Lou seemed my reward for enduring my upbringing. I was convinced of this now that I had returned to my roots. My parents didn't miss a step in recognizing her as a kindred spirit from their childhood, someone striving to better herself with the acceptance that life was hard even if she felt like she was the bottom of the barrel as far as social class was concerned.

My parents during the Depression felt like the bottom of the barrel, and for good reason. They *were* the bottom of the barrel. But everyone had to survive anyway. Life was cruel, even if some had it worse than others. I adored how my parents warmed to Mary Lou. As if she were a prize to them for their raising of me. And she responded to their warmth by fitting into our life together as we lived it.

Our house had air conditioning. It was one of the first in our region to have it. I hated the artificial air, however. I preferred a fan, but my parents were middle class now and sick of a lifetime of heat and more heat. Texas heat. Damned heat. Once they had any money at all, they'd built the brick house we all now lived in. This occurred when I was two years old. I had no memories of the old wooden house they'd lived in during the early years of their marriage. The tile floor and open screened windows kept our brick house livable even with the Texas heat. Fans made it even seem comfortable.

But as soon as central air conditioning reached the Rio Grande Valley, my successful farmer of a dad had it installed in our house. I never got used to it and thought I might freeze to death right in the middle of summer. I began to sleep at night out in our front yard because of it. A blanket spread out in our front yard under a big ash tree was perfect. And it made me feel more like a rural Texan, too. Davy Crockett wouldn't be caught dead in an air-conditioned house, I was certain. It helped get some of my self-esteem back during the times my parents derided me for not being up to their childhood memories.

And now I shared this front yard environment with Mary Lou, the girl from the deserts of Tucson. Talk about getting back to nature! You could hear the birds chirping from the trees around. You could see the stars gleaming all throughout the sky as we lay on our backs before dozing off. The moon seemed like a spotlight with its brightness upon us as if we were the center of attention.

"We have mild winters here, as you've noticed," I

explained to Mary Lou as we lay on top of our sleeping bags in our front yard one night. "Sometimes a norther blows in and it gets cold. I considered it cold, anyway, before living up north during their winter months. But every few years it even froze here. My sleeping bag was up to that cold, but my daddy wouldn't let me sleep out in rain or very cold weather. The yard is an acre and our front yard is pretty far from the highway, so we weren't concerned with bad guys. My father is a good shot, too. Just in case harmful elements encroached. I love it out here, especially under this ash tree. You've experienced plowing at night and loved it, so I hope you love it out here now. You don't have to do this with me. If you prefer sleeping inside, we can. I want you to be comfortable and happy."

"This is wonderful, Kaleb," she replied. "We lived in towns. I remember small towns, back before Mother moved us to Tucson. But it never crossed our minds to camp out in any yard. This is so peaceful. And yes, the night air is marvelous. The air conditioner doesn't get to me like it does you, but it is so nice out here—and especially romantic with you."

"Speaking of romance," I said. "When *should* we start a family? Meaning 'have kids.' You're still taking classes. I don't want that interrupted. My mother could help raise our kids, though. Mom and Dad will even welcome that—you've heard them talk."

"I don't know, Kaleb. I do think about it. But yes, like you said, I have school to attend and want to take as many classes as I can. Pan Am is harder than anything at Southmost, and I want to be sure to keep good grades. And yes, I would like to get a job after graduation, in real estate to put my schooling to good use. But we shouldn't wait too long. Especially so Mother and Pops won't be too old. For their sake as grandparents, and for our kids' sake, you know, to have active grandparents for them to know and appreciate."

"Yeah," I said with a sigh. "I know we say this every time we talk about it. But I want to bring it up now and then to see if that's still how you see it."

"It's so good here, Kaleb. Even the hardships. They don't seem hardships as much as just everyday life with obstacles to help build our character. We can handle it all. Up to now anyway. And I want to have a job for a few years too, to develop my skill and get a bit of money. Even send a bit more money home to my mom. I feel the same way every time we talk about it."

"It seems like fate, doesn't it, Mary Lou? Us meeting and working all these things out. It seems like some life roadmap. Here we are. We followed the map and it led us to our destination."

"It does seem like fate, Kaleb. I am so reassured about my life. About myself as a person, too. It makes me want to be the best wife in the world and best mother in the world. I want the world to have more like us. Citizens of fate. Ready to raise kids to pass it on through the ages. I never thought these kinds of thoughts before, Kaleb. But we didn't dream any of this up. The yellow brick road we've travelled laid it out perfectly for us."

Chapter Twenty-Five

Though we didn't make much money off our few head of livestock, raising them made me feel the full brunt of being a Texan. They were domestic livestock for our own consumption—five head of cattle, two pigs, four goats, five chickens and one rooster that we raised in our fenced-in pasture that surrounded a cattle tank supplying water. The cotton, vegetables, and grain from our fields were our cash crops. Mary Lou helped my mother make butter from the milk of our cows and our goats. They used the same churn my mother had used as a little girl during the Depression. We had more eggs than we needed, so we let a few from each batch grow into chickens to eat, rather than buy any in supermarkets. I still didn't relish snapping their necks and pulling out all the feathers. That part made me at least consider buying their meat instead of raising it ourselves.

And I still was not a good mechanic. As a boy, I assumed I would grow into being a good mechanic someday. Every farmer I ever met was a good mechanic, for time-saving and convenience as well as not spending money on repair shops. But I never got the hang of anything about maintenance and repair. As a Marine, my mechanical aptitude was so low they would not let me have a military driver's license. Somehow God overlooked me when competence was passed out for anything mechanical. My father routinely repaired our equipment, and I was stuck with helping him. If it was a problem he knew he'd put a lot of time into, he would indeed take it to a tractor dealer for repair. But there were constant small repairs and adjustments to make on our machines, and I had to help him with them. I admired my father and other farmers for being so self-sufficient, but I was sure I would never be up to any of this if left to myself.

Nor was I good in Spanish. My father had a very poor educational background, but he could make the farm run and handle the business end, too—including talks in fluent Spanish with our Mexican workers. If I had not excelled in school, I would have grown up with severe doubts about my intelligence. Even knowing I was good at seemingly everything else in life, having such severe flaws on our farm still attacked my ego quite often. My father had little respect for formal education—book learning, as he called it—when he saw my flaws on the farm.

I worried about any children I might bring into this world. Would they take after me concerning mechanical aptitude? My father would be totally retired from the farm by the time they took over. But maybe some of them would develop mechanical abilities from helping him before he got too old.

"Guess what I heard on the radio on the way home from Pan Am?" Mary Lou asked one day with a tease. She stared at me as I blankly stared back at her. "Come on, Kaleb, go for it. Why would I care enough to ask you if it wasn't a big deal? Do I ever ask a question like this? Give it a shot."

I thought for a moment, trying to picture why she would care.

"Buffy Sainte-Marie?" I asked. "Our song, maybe? 'Take My Hand for a While'?"

"Bingo!" she chirped. "I was so excited. Why do we never hear this song? It's from the sixties, but it was a big hit for both Buffy Sainte-Marie and Glen Campbell. Anyway, I got flutters inside while listening to it. You know, we have to order that somewhere. It's never in stores anywhere or on any oldies albums. Never on the radio or television. I'm bugged now and can't believe we didn't get a copy of it back in Tucson. Anyway, I'm going to order it. They have all these oldies companies that sell these things. We're not spending another anniversary without playing that song. If not a record version, they have to have it on cassettes. They have everything on cassettes now, it seems."

She leaned over to place a juicy kiss on my lips. It was like we were still in the first throes of our love.

"So what are you doing home so early?" Mary Lou asked me. "I thought you were in the fields, chiseling."

"Daddy needed help getting a tractor tire changed. He had a flat in the twenty acres near Primera. There was a spike in the ground he was unearthing, and it poked a big hole in one of the back tractor tires. You know, one of those big ones where the side fenders cover them. Where we sit sometimes when one of us is riding."

"I know what you're talking about, Kaleb. I've been helping you drive tractors for over a year now. What do you think of me?"

"Dad's getting up in years, and the two of us barely got that tire pulled off, there in the field, and rolled into the back of the pickup. I just got home. I'm through for the day. Let the tractor shop fix that thing, and Dad and I will put it back on the tractor tomorrow. It was hell getting that spike out of the ground. It was buried below the surface. Maybe it's been there for years and we've just been missing it somehow as we work there with our tractors. But it finally got us. The flood we had last month probably surfaced it a bit. I had to take a chain and pull it out with the tractor that had the flat tire. I don't know what it's from. Anyway, here I am to greet you. And what are you beaming about? Did you ace another test? Don't you get sick of making A's?"

"I'll never get sick of making A's, Kaleb. And yes, I made an A minus on my microeconomics test. One of the few A's on this test. Our prof is hard core. He wants us to learn economics. He thinks voters vote in too many bad politicians that don't know diddly-squat about the economy."

"Or politicians who don't care about what they do know if they can get elected by voters wanting a handout. As if that's going to help anyone when we run out of money from all these handouts."

"You got the gist of it, Kaleb. My prof really likes me. He likes that I want to get into real estate and wants to help me. Maybe he'll recommend me someday."

"You're set to graduate next year," I remarked. "He'll still remember you if he's so keen on you."

I stared at her inquisitively for a moment.

"I'm all for you getting out into the big world, Mary Lou. We've talked about it. But you'll need to work full time for at least two years to get your craft down as a real estate agent. But when are we going to have kids?"

"We can have them, can't we?" she mused in return. "Your parents can take care of them while you and I work. We even still live in the same house with them. Yes, just like we've decided every time you bring it up."

"Yep," I replied with a nod. "But I'm still wondering how snug you're going to get in real estate. You'll be good—and I want you to be. I'm not just saying that because you keep making the Dean's list. You've got a knack and now you've got all this self-confidence. I'm thinking there will be no turning back for you."

"Kaleb, even if that's true, Mother and Pops can help us with the kids. That will free a lot of time up. We keep going over all this. What's your problem?"

"They're getting old, Mary Lou. They've raised kids before, but now, even with us helping them, they soon won't have the patience. It's unfair to ask much help from them when we finally do have kids."

"That's true, Kaleb. But working full time in real estate will let me send more money to my mother and sister. It's all complicated, but we're in the 1980s now, and it's an ever-evolving world. We'll do what we have to do. At least we have a game plan, for now. And with me supplementing our family income, we can make a decent living. Farming is so unpredictable, and it's becoming more so. We'll have two breadwinners. We'll just have to respond to our circumstances as we face them. We already know our direction. That's all we can do for now."

She was right. There would be more talks in the future. We had to stay focused and make everything work. Including our marriage.

Chapter Twenty-Six

"I have to stay focused for one more week," Mary Lou said to us at the supper table. "Next week is dead week, and I have to push myself. I'm so burnt out, but I can feel victory—A's in all my subjects and if I pass these last quizzes, I won't have to take finals. And I'll do it! Even if I lose my A's I'll still pass my courses. So, no finals for graduating seniors unless they need to get their final grade up to passing. I've come this far, I'm an honor student, and it's time to go out in a blaze of glory!"

"Did you talk to that agency, the real estate guy you interviewed with?" my father asked. "How soon can you start work with him after graduation?"

"Within the week," Mary Lou replied. "I get a couple of days off first, though. I'm glad for the days off, but I'm interested in my new job. My first professional job! I'll learn the ropes as soon as possible and get my mindset right. But a couple of days off is great. I'm so sick of studying. Just let me take the real estate test and get my license, all while this is fresh on my mind. I should do okay."

"You'll do great, Mary Lou. You never struggle anymore. Not like when we were in Tucson, when we first met. Those days when you were afraid to go to class are ancient history. You had no confidence back then."

"I had confidence from the beginning," she replied. "After meeting you, anyway. But I had to learn how to study. How to psych my mind into it. But then I didn't really struggle anymore after I finally got my bearings."

"You know," my mother said, "you hear about the land of opportunity. America, you know. But you had to go get that opportunity, Mary Lou. To actually do it. You were the poster girl for all that. Once you got a whiff of things, once you got your focus and direction, there was no stopping you."

"Oh, thank you, Mother!" Mary Lou gazed at her affectionately. "I would never have become an honor student if not for Kaleb, and then y'all with your encouragement. It shocked me to find myself, but then it shocked me more that I hadn't found myself sooner. We can do this. This is America. We have to be the ones that do it, but there is all this opportunity for us to do it. All this network and environment."

"You'll be the perfect mother," my father praised. "Y'all will be wonderful parents."

She *was* going to be the perfect mother. That was wonderful to hear, but now as I approached my mid-thirties, the longing to start our own personal family was gnawing at me. As much as I wanted to be supportive of her finding herself and having a successful career, just when would children fit into her plans? There were couples we'd met sometimes who had this as an issue, with the husband demanding children while the wife was into her career. Sometimes turmoil on the subject led to divorce. I just knew it was better to be patient and to see her happy and seeking success.

It became more complex once she began her new job in the real estate world. Questioning how little I saw of Mary Lou now that she was full throttle into her new job bothered my conscience. At least when she was a college student I was more involved in her life. Now she carried her new job into her private hours even when she was at home. I was lonely now. Even with my parents around.

The Christmas season helped ease this loneliness. Mary Lou loved Christmas as much as anyone—the decorations and music, the good wishes from so many. But she was still gone much of the time and busy with the job even while at home. A "don't bother me" busy. The loneliness inside me only got lonelier, with longing even to share a TV movie with her. But there was always some prospect for a real estate sale she had to worry about even while at home. Her job was like living in a foreign country for me. We could communicate, back when she was a student. She sometimes needed me as an emotional crutch then. Real estate, though, was like she was in another part of our lives…without me.

"You make me feel like we're roommates," I whined one night after she got home in the early evening yet again.

"Kaleb," she groaned, "we've been through this before. We haven't talked about it for a few weeks and I was hoping maybe it was finally settled. There are so many things to do, and often times it takes extra effort on some of the deals. Or potential deals. I can't just desert my clients or the company that pays me. And I'm still proving myself. I've pretty much proven myself, but that can vanish really quickly if I don't work hard. There's no room to blow a deal."

"I still feel like your roommate. So that's my side."

"But somehow you can keep farming," she came back with a bite.

"Me being a farmer never caused us problems, especially when you were with me in the pickup or on a tractor. It felt like a family farm even when you were in the house. I barely feel like your husband now, even when we're home together. Should I quit the farm and be bored sitting around just hoping to see you? May as well farm, since I seldom see you anyway."

She started to say something but held back. After a blunt stare she turned and walked away to the bedroom and slammed the door behind her. I considered sleeping on the couch but that was too much like brooding. Somehow, this had to be worked out.

I wanted a distraction from my row with Mary Lou, but I couldn't concentrate on anything but our problem. I considered again trying to be understanding, to appreciate her need for accomplishment, even for women being successful in the workplace. But family mattered to me. That was a good cause too.

I walked to our bedroom and tested the doorknob quietly to see if it was locked. The door opened. She lay asleep in bed, but with the night light turned on nearby. Perhaps a good sign.

I made my way slowly to our bed and took my clothes off, laying them in the chair near the nightstand before crawling in next to her. While closing my eyes, I felt her hand touch my cheek and I turned to look at her.

"I'm not selling out my cause," she told me sweetly, "but I don't mean to hurt you. It's selfish of me to ignore our marriage so much. I tried to think of you as the one being selfish, which you can be, but no more than me. We presented our case with each other. Now it's time to save our marriage."

It felt marvelous to feel married again. Like someone had waved some magic wand.

She looked me directly in the eyes. "When entering

the room after our fight," she began, "I turned on the radio hoping not to hear anything else you might say. Not to be provoked into continuing the fight. And you won't believe it, but instantly—literally instantly!—the opening words of 'Take My Hand for a While' were on, but sung this time by Glen Campbell. It came through as if it was you singing to me because of your broken heart. And I cried. Absolutely cried tears into my pillow. It's still moist from those tears. Do you believe in fate, Kaleb? I sort of do sometimes, but it seems superstitious to do that, so I tried to talk myself out of it. But this was God somehow. And the significance of Glen Campbell singing it, you know, singing it to me *personally* somehow… As if it was *you* singing to me. Telling me to take your hand. Like in the song. For the sake of your broken heart."

She stroked my cheek softly once more.

"Oh, Kaleb! Nothing is more important than us. Than you and me. Married. Married in every sense of the word. Somehow this wasn't Buffy Sainte-Marie or Glen Campbell. This was God. I really literally believe this was God."

I kissed her on the lips softly and stroked her cheek as she had done mine.

"I could stop farming, Mary Lou. Maybe get a good job somewhere. There aren't that many good jobs around, though, and I've been out of the workforce so long. All I have to show is that I've got a college degree, been a Marine, and been a farmer. There probably are some agriculturally related agencies around that would hire me. But we'd have to give up the farm. The family farm. That would kill my parents. But even then I'd come home to nothing. Nothing except not even a farm. Just two roommates working separate jobs."

"They are *our* parents," she corrected.

I nodded in approval at her admonition and stroked her cheek again.

"It's good you want to talk about it," I said. "Let's try to be fair with each other, but not just give in. Let's find a solution."

"I've formed some ideas," she told me. "Not as a solution to our conflict, but about my place in the workforce. To find answers for us, too. Our marriage. Our situation. I've been a real estate agent for two years. Give me another year with my employer. That will get me established enough to go independent. I'll make my own way alone. It may mean quitting work during the day after only three hours or perhaps five. That way we could have children. It wouldn't just be dumping any children on Mother and Pops. In fact, let's plan for a baby. In about six months or so we can plan for a pregnancy. Whenever I do get pregnant, I'll close off whatever I have going with the agency and bear the child, and nurse and raise it for a couple of years. After that I can be an independent agent and work three-hour days or whatever. I'm ready to be a mother now. It's pushing at me, inside. My biological clock is ticking. I've been enjoying my new world here so far, but now I want a family. And to be your wife again."

"I can help raise our child," I replied, feeling the same emotion. "There are peak seasons on the farm and sometimes work will be demanding. But there are slack times, too. This country has been hands-on agricultural for so long, but we have machines now that can cut our work hours down from what they used to be. We'll get it done."

"It's like we still care about each other," she said endearingly. "I've missed it. I've been distracted. I understand why and don't feel all wrong. There's this need to succeed. But now we need better ideas and solutions."

"This could have gotten bad if we didn't solve it," I said. "Caring about each other did the solving. I'm almost glad this happened. Maybe we were just a little too happy before. It was too easy. We needed this test, to prove ourselves to each other, and we passed this test. Well, sort of. We have to follow through. But we will. We'll take each other's hands for a while longer."

Chapter Twenty-Seven

I smiled down at Mary Lou and our new son, Blevin. She was the most beautiful I had ever seen her. Even now, after giving birth to our firstborn. I thought back to the movie *Hawaii* when Max Von Sydow's character beholds his son for the first time and declares in a burst of emotion how he loves his wife more than God. A blasphemous statement, especially for a preacher.

I didn't want to blaspheme God myself. But as red and wrinkled as Blevin was when I saw him for the first time, not even an hour old, and with Mary Lou so haggard and exhausted, I was sure no bigger wonderment existed in the world. Nor could I picture more beauty than when I beheld her.

"A girl would have been nice," I told her. "You deserve a girl for all you've done. All your problems with pregnancy, and the tortures of labor as you bore our son just now. But I have to admit, a son leaves me proud."

"It should be a son," she said barely easing into a smile. "For you. You've done so much for me. So much. You deserve to have a son. And you let me name him. Thank you. My aunt on my mother's side—you never met her, I'm sorry to say—she married a man whose last name was Blevins. I fell in love with that name for some reason. And when searching for names her last name from her husband came to mind. So, I dropped the s to where it almost sounds like a first name. Perhaps, anyway."

"It's good he's a boy so he can inherit our farm someday," I said with a sigh.

"Have you told Mother and Pops?" she asked me.

"Of course. Yes. They were so good about not offering any names. I even wanted them to. But they were so thrilled to finally be grandparents they wanted you to name our child unimpeded. So gracious of them. They seem to love the name Blevin. I'm sure they do. But they would pretend to do so even if somehow they don't."

She looked at me with affection.

"All this makes me happy, Kaleb," she said just above a whisper. "I know I *should* be happy, but I really *am* happy. I still don't believe in fate, but I don't disbelieve it either. I was so down and out, growing up, more emotionally than anything, but especially about my life, my status, or for any hope. I was simply trying to exist. Then you came."

"And you know the rest of the story," I replied. "You entered my life right back. Not just loving me and appreciating me, but needing me to need you. We fed on each other. I'm so glad I helped you find yourself. Is it biblical or karmic or fate or what? All the above, perhaps. But here we are. And still so in love. It does seem like fate to me. Too real to be just coincidental. But I'm glad we don't know if it's fate or not. I quit thinking for a while about it being fate and that kept me searching for answers. I'm glad for the search for answers, but it still seems like fate even after all the search."

"Answers are wonderful," she returned. "And we do keep finding them. I still think about my career and care about it. But I love being a woman, a wife, and now a mother. And it matters to me. I'm no feminist, yet I appreciate a woman's place in the modern world, and it thrills me to be a part of that modern world. I'm focused on motherhood now, however. I suppose that makes sense and is natural. And like Jackie Kennedy said, motherhood is the most important role for a woman. I guess I'm paraphrasing. I haven't worked as a real estate agent for very long, and not as an independent one. Right now it's the furthest thing from my mind. But I'll want it again someday. To make my way, to find personal fulfillment in this modern world and also to contribute to the family. Financially and all, you know. Perhaps I could go back to helping on the farm some, and help that way. But probably I'll want to be an independent agent again. So much to sort out. I at least have skills and confidence. I so want Blevin's happiness and to help him grow and mature. We have so much to teach him. It's wonderful to have so much to contribute to him. Not just as a loving mother, but as someone who can show him the way from my experiences. Including in the big economic world out there. There's so much for me to offer now from all I've learned. And it all started with you. You. The one God sent to me."

"Our first child is a boy," I noted. "We'll start him on the farm early. Like my dad did with me. He can ride around in the pickup and be with me for some of the work that's less demanding. He can be in the fields with both of us when we have to get rid of weeds and haul equipment from one place to another. He can start driving a small tractor as early as elementary school. Help with irrigation. A farm is more family-oriented than crop-oriented. It's more important for growing a family than for producing cash crops. I'm so glad there are still some family farms around. I love progress, and it's good America has moved on from an agricultural stage into an industrial power and even into a hi-tech power. But I miss the family-oriented farms and farming communities. Maybe that's what Heaven is. With the big *patrón* being God. No idea how this stuff works, but I love the thought."

"Stay a while, Kaleb." She beckoned me. "There's nothing pressing you, is there?"

I shook my head no.

"Mom and Dad have it under control. Harvest is over. The hard work is over for a while. The pressing stuff, anyway."

"Could you spend the night?" she asked longingly. "I'll feel lonely except that I have Blevin here. But in some ways, it will be lonely *because* of him, too. With you not here to share, you know."

"Mom and Dad want to come see you tonight," I said. "They are so excited being grandparents. They lived to see the day. I better go back now. There's a lot to tend to. I'll let you be with them and with Blevin tonight. It will be more meaningful for them to concentrate on you and our son alone. We'll share all this together soon enough. I'm so glad we still live with them in the same house. Family is everything."

Mary Lou and I stared at each other starry-eyed in a moment of awareness. "And Kaleb," Mary Lou said as I turned to leave, "you took my hand for a while. And look what it gave us."

A word about the author...

Born in Harlingen, Texas on October 7, 1948 where I grew up and worked on a cotton farm, I graduated from Harlingen High School in 1966. I attended Texas A&M beginning in Summer 1966. In January 1970 I dropped out to enlist in the United States Marine Corps, where I served as an enlisted man, attaining the rank of Sergeant, with an honorable discharge after three years. I worked as a computer programmer afterwards in Houston and as a civil servant for a US Air Force Base in Frankfurt, Germany. I traveled and worked in Europe for two years, which included flying to Israel in October 1973 to aid the Jewish State in the Yom Kippor War. I was also in Greece in the summer of 1974 when the war between Greece and Turkey erupted over Cyprus. I was stuck on the Greek island of Ios for part of that war until I managed to catch a boat to Athens just in time to watch the Greek military dictatorship fold. I returned to Texas A&M in the fall of 1976 to finish my bachelor's degree in Business Management. I went back to Europe afterwards and also to Israel where I lived for almost a year. I later taught English in Taiwan before returning home in 1980 to get a master's degree in Agricultural Economics, received in 1982. I joined the US Peace Corps in 1984 and served for three years in the Philippines. In 1987 I began work for the Swiss government as a computer programmer until 1998. I have worked in the IT department of Texas A&M since 1998. I have three children and am presently divorced. I am Jewish.

Thank you for purchasing
this publication of The Wild Rose Press, Inc.

For questions or more information
contact us at
info@thewildrosepress.com.

The Wild Rose Press, Inc.
www.thewildrosepress.com